Children Is All

Children
Is
All

By James Purdy

A NEW DIRECTIONS BOOK

Some of the stories in this book have appeared in the following magazines
and anthologies, to whom we give grateful thanks for permission to re-
print: *Commentary, Esquire, New Directions 17, New World Writing 17,
Partisan Review,* and *The Texas Quarterly.* "About Jessie Mae" first
appeared, in altered form, in *The New Yorker.*

CAUTION: Professionals and amateurs are hereby warned that "Children Is
All" and "Cracks," being fully protected under the copyright laws of the
United States of America, the British Empire, including the Dominion of
Canada, and all other countries of the world, are subject to royalty. All
rights, including professional, amateur, motion picture, recitation, lectur-
ing, public reading, radio broadcasting, television, and the rights of trans-
lation into foreign languages are strictly reserved. Permission must be
secured from the author's representative, Gilbert Parker, Curtis Brown,
Ltd., 60 East 56th Street, New York 10022.

Manufactured in the United States of America
First published clothbound in 1962
First published as ND Paperbook 327 in 1971
Published simultaneously in Canada by McClelland & Stewart, Ltd.

New Directions Books are published for James Laughlin
by New Directions Publishing Corporation,
333 Sixth Avenue, New York 10014

for John Bucklew

and Bruce Ross, thanks.

Contents

Stories

Plays

Stories

Daddy Wolf

You aren't the first man to ask me what I am doing so long in the phone booth with the door to my flat open and all. Let me explain something, or if you want to use the phone, I'll step out for a minute, but I am trying to get Operator to re-connect me with a party she just cut me off from. If you're not in a big hurry would you let me just try to get my party again.

See I been home 2 days now just looking at them 2 or 3 holes in the linoleum in my flat, and those holes are so goddam big now—you can go in there and take a look—those holes are so goddam big that I bet my kid, if he was still here, could almost put his leg through the biggest one.

Maybe of course the rats don't use the linoleum holes as entrances or exits. They could come through the calcimine in the wall. But I kind of guess and I bet the super for once would back me up on this, the rats are using the linoleum holes. Otherwise what is the meaning of the little black specks in and near each hole in the linoleum. I don't see how you could ignore the black specks there. If they were using the wall holes you would expect black specks there, but I haven't found a single one.

The party I was just talking to on the phone when I got

3

cut off was surprised when I told her how the other night after my wife and kid left me I came in to find myself staring right head-on at a fat, I guess a Mama rat, eating some of my uncooked cream of wheat. I was so took by surprise that I did not see which way she went out. She ran, is all I can say, the minute I come into the room.

I had no more snapped back from seeing the Mama rat when a teeny baby one run right between my legs and disappeared ditto.

I just stood looking at my uncooked cream of wheat knowing I would have to let it go to waste.

It was too late that evening to call the super or anybody and I know from a lot of sad experience how sympathetic he would be, for the rats, to quote him, is a *un-avoidable probability* for whatever party decides to rent one of these you-know-what linoleum apartments.

If you want something better than some old you-know-what linoleum-floor apartments, the super says, *you got the map of Newyorkcity to hunt with.*

Rats and linoleum go together, and when you bellyache about rats, remember you're living on linoleum.

I always have to go to the hall phone when I get in one of these states, but tonight instead of calling the super who has gone off by now anyhow to his night job (he holds down 2 jobs on account of, he says, the high cost of chicken and peas), I took the name of the first party my finger fell on in the telephone book.

This lady answered the wire.

I explained to her the state I was in, and that I was over in one of the linoleum apartments and my wife and kid left me.

She cleared her throat and so on.

Even for a veteran, I told her, this is rough.

She kind of nodded over the phone in her manner.

I could feel she was sort of half-friendly, and I told her how I had picked her name out from all the others in the telephone book.

It was rough enough, I explained to her, to be renting an apartment in the linoleum district and to not know nobody in Newyorkcity, and then only the other night after my wife and kid left me this Mama rat was in here eating my uncooked cream of wheat, and before I get over this, her offspring run right between my legs.

This lady on the wire seemed to say *I see* every so often but I couldn't be sure on account of I was talking so fast myself.

I would have called the super of the building, I explained to her, in an emergency like this, but he has 2 jobs, and as it is after midnight now he is on his night job. But it would be just as bad in the daytime as then usually he is out inspecting the other linoleum apartments or catching up on his beauty sleep and don't answer the door or phone.

When I first moved into this building, I told her, I had to pinch myself to be sure I was actually seeing it right. I seen all the dirt before I moved in, but once I was in, I really SEEN: all the traces of the ones who had been here before, people who had died or lost their jobs or found they was the wrong race or something and had had to vacate all of a sudden before they could clean the place up for the next tenant. A lot of them left in such a hurry they just give you a present of some of their belongings and underwear along with their dirt. But then after one party left in such a hurry, somebody else from somewhere moved in, found he could not make it in Newyorkcity, and lit out somewhere or maybe was taken to a hospital in a serious condition and never returned.

I moved in just like the others on the linoleum.

Wish you could have seen it then. Holes everywhere and that most jagged of the holes I can see clear over here from the phone booth is where the Mama rat come through, which seems now about 3,000 years ago to me.

I told the lady on the phone how polite she was to go on listening and I hoped I was not keeping her up beyond her bedtime or from having a nightcap before she did turn in.

I don't object to animals, see. If it had been a Mama bird, say, which had come out of the hole, I would have had a start, too, as a Mama bird seldom is about and around at that hour, not to mention it not nesting in a linoleum hole, but I think I feel the way I do just because you think of rats along with neglect and lonesomeness and not having nobody near or around you.

See my wife left me and took our kid with her. They could not take any more of Newyorkcity. My wife was very scared of disease, and she had heard the radio in a shoe-repair store telling that they were going to raise the V.D. rate, and she said to me just a few hours before she left, *I don't think I am going to stay on here, Benny, if they are going to have one of them health epidemics*. She didn't have a disease, but she felt she would if the city officials were bent on raising the V.D. rate. She said it would be her luck and she would be no exception to prove the rule. She packed and left with the kid.

Did I feel sunk with them gone, but Jesus it was all I could do to keep on here myself. A good number of times at night I did not share my cream of wheat with them. I told them to prepare what kind of food they had a yen for and let me eat my cream of wheat alone with a piece of warmed-over oleo and just a sprinkle of brown sugar on that.

My wife and kid would stand and watch me eat the

cream of wheat, but they was entirely indifferent to food.
I think it was partly due to the holes in the linoleum, and
them knowing what was under the holes of course.

We have only the one chair in the flat, and so my kid
never had any place to sit when I was to home.

I couldn't help telling this party on the phone then
about my wife and DADDY WOLF.

I was the one who told my wife about DADDY WOLF and
the TROUBLE PHONE in the first place, but at first she said
she didn't want any old charity no matter if it was money
or advice or just encouraging words.

Then when things got so rough, my wife did call DADDY
WOLF. I think the number is CRack 8-7869 or something
like that, and only ladies can call. You phone this number
and say *Daddy Wolf, I am a lady in terrible trouble. I am
in one of the linoleum apartments, and just don't feel I
can go on another day. Mama rats are coming in and out of
their holes with their babies, and all we have had to eat in
a month is cream of wheat.*

DADDY WOLF would say he was listening and to go on,
and then he would ask her if she was employed anywhere.

DADDY WOLF, *yes and no. I just do not seem to have the
willpower to go out job-hunting any more or on these
house-to-house canvassing jobs that I have been holding
down lately, and if you could see this linoleum flat, I think
you would agree, DADDY WOLF, that there is very little
incentive for me and Benny.*

Then my wife would go on about how surprised we had
both been, though she was the only one surprised, over the
high rate of V.D. in Newyorkcity.

*You see, DADDY WOLF, I won't hold a thing back, I have
been about with older men in order to tide my husband
over this rough financial situation we're in. My husband*

*works in the mitten factory, and he just is not making
enough for the three of us to live on. He has to have his
cream of wheat at night or he would not have the strength
to go back to his day-shift, and our linoleum apartment
costs 30 smackers a week.*

*I leave the kid alone here and go out to try and find
work,* DADDY WOLF, *but I'm telling you, the only job I can
find for a woman of my education and background is this
house-to-house canvassing of Queen Bee royal jelly which
makes older women look so much more appealing, but I
hardly sell more than a single jar a day and am on my feet
12 hours at a stretch.*

*The kid is glad when I go out to sell as he can have the
chair to himself then. You see when I and his Daddy are
home he either has to sit down on my lap, if I am sitting,
or if his Daddy is sitting, just stand because I won't allow
a little fellow like him to sit on that linoleum, it's not safe,
and his Daddy will not let him sit on his lap because he is
too dead-tired from the mitten factory.*

That was the way she explained to DADDY WOLF on the
TROUBLE PHONE, and that went on every night, night after
night, until she left me.

DADDY WOLF always listened, I will give him credit for
that. He advised Mabel too: *go to Sunday school and
church and quit going up to strange men's hotel rooms.
Devote yourself only to your husband's need, and you don't
ever have to fear the rise in the V.D. rate.*

My wife, though, could just not take Newyorkcity. She
was out selling that Queen Bee royal jelly every day, but
when cold weather come she had only a thin coat and she
went out less and less and that all added up to less cream of
wheat for me in the evening.

It is funny thing about cream of wheat, you don't get

tired of it. I think if I ate, say, hamburger and chop suey
every night, I would get sick and tired of them. Not that
I ever dine on them. But if I did, I would—get sick and
tired, I mean. But there's something about cream of wheat,
with just a daub of warm oleo on it, and a sprinkle of
brown sugar that makes you feel you might be eatin' it for
the first time.

My wife don't care for cream of wheat nearly so much as
I do.

Our kid always ate with the old gentleman down the hall
with the skullcap. He rung a bell when it was supper time,
and the kid went down there and had his meal. Once in a
while, he brought back something or other for us.

It's funny talking to you like this, Mister, and as I told
this lady I am waiting to get re-connected with on the
phone, if I didn't know any better I would think either one
of you was DADDY WOLF on the TROUBLE PHONE.

Well, Mabel left me, then, and took the kid with her.

It was her silly fear of the V.D. rate that really made her
light out. She could have stayed here indefinitely. She
loved this here city at first. She was just crazy about Central
Park.

Newyorkcity was just the place for me to find work in.
I had a good job with the Singer sewing-machine people in
one of their spare-parts rooms, then I got laid off and was
without a thing for over 6 months and then was lucky to
find this job at the mitten factory. I raise the lever that sews
the inner lining to your mittens.

I don't think it is Mabel and the kid leaving me so much
sometimes as it is the idea of that Mama rat coming
through the holes in the linoleum that has got me so down-
in-the-dumps today. I didn't even go to the mitten factory
this A.M., and I have, like I say, got so down-in-the-dumps I

almost felt like calling DADDY WOLF myself on the
TROUBLE PHONE like she did all the time. But knowing he
won't talk to nobody but ladies, as a kind of next-best-thing
I put my finger down haphazard on top of this lady's name
in the phone book, and I sure appreciated having that talk
with her.

See DADDY WOLF would only talk with my wife for about
one and a half minutes on account of other women were
waiting to tell him their troubles. He would always say
*Go back to your affiliation with the Sunday school and
church of your choice, Mabel, and you'll find your burdens
lighter in no time.*

DADDY said the same thing to her every night, but she
never got tired hearing it, I guess.

DADDY WOLF told Mabel she didn't have to have any fear
at all of the V.D. rate on account of she was a married
woman and therefore did not have to go out for that relationship, but if she ever felt that DESIRE coming over her
when her husband was gone, to just sit quiet and read an
uplifting book.

Mabel has not had time, I don't think, to write me yet,
taking care of the kid and all, and getting settled back
home, and I have, well, been so goddam worried about
everything. They are talking now about a shut-down at the
mitten factory so that I hardly as a matter of fact have had
time to think about my wife and kid, let alone miss them.
There is, as a matter of fact, more cream of wheat now for
supper, and I splurged today and bought a 5-pound box of
that soft brown sugar that don't turn to lumps, which I
wouldn't ever have done if they was still here.

The old gent down the hall with the skullcap misses my
kid, as he almost entirely kept the boy in eats.

He never speaks to me in the hall, the old man. They

said, I heard this somewhere, he don't have linoleum on his floor, but carpets, but I have not been invited in to see.

This building was condemned two years ago, but still isn't torn down, and the old man is leaving as soon as he can find the right neighborhood for his married daughter to visit him in.

Wait a minute. No, I thought I seen some action from under that one hole there in the linoleum.

Excuse me if I have kept you from using the phone with my talk but all I can say is you and this lady on the phone have been better for me tonight than DADDY WOLF on the TROUBLE PHONE ever was for my wife.

Up until now I have usually called the super when I was in one of these down-moods, but all he ever said was *Go back where you and Mabel got your own people and roots, Benny. You can't make it here in a linoleum apartment with your background and education.*

He has had his eyes opened—the super. He has admitted himself that he never thought Mabel and me could stick it out this long. (He don't know she is gone.)

But I won't give up. I WILL NOT give up. Mabel let a thing like the hike in the V.D. rates chase her out. I tried to show her that that was just statistics, but she always was superstitious as all get-out.

I judge when this scare I've had about the Mama rat dies down and I get some sleep and tomorrow if I go back to the mitten factory I will then really and truly begin to miss Mabel and the kid. The old man down the hall already misses the kid. That kid ate more in one meal with him than Mabel and me eat the whole week together. I don't begrudge it to him, though, because he was growing.

Well, Mister, if you don't want to use the phone after all, I think I will try to have Operator re-connect me with that party I got disconnected from. I guess as this is the hour that Mabel always called DADDY WOLF I have just automatically caught her habit, and anyhow I sure felt in the need of a talk.

Do you hear that funny clicking sound? Here, I'll hold you the receiver so as you can hear it. Don't go away just yet: I think Operator is getting me that party again, so stick around awhile yet.

No, they cut us off again, hear? there is a bad connection or something.

Well, like I say, anyhow Mabel and the kid did get out of here, even if it was superstition. Christ, when I was a boy I had every one of those diseases and it never did me no hurt. I went right into the army with a clean bill of health, Korea, home again, and now Newyorkcity.

You can't bullshit me with a lot of statistics.

Mabel, though, goddam it, I could knock the teeth down her throat, running out on me like this and taking the kid.

WHERE IS THAT GODDAM OPERATOR?

Hello. Look, Operator, what number was that I dialed and talked so long. Re-connect me please. That number I just got through talking with so long. I don't know the party's name or number. Just connect me back, will you please. This here is an emergency phone call, Operator.

Home by Dark

Every day his grandfather bought him a new toy of a cheap kind, and a little racing car made out of chocolate. The boy ate the racing car slowly and almost dutifully as he and his grandfather sat on the immense porch and talked about how the birds know when to leave for the South.

"Have we ever been South?" the boy asked his grandfather, after he had finished the chocolate racing car and wiped his hands carefully on his cowboy handkerchief.

"No," the old man said. "Not since your parents died."

"Why don't we go?" the young boy said.

"There would be no reason to," the old man replied.

The birds that had been twittering on the huge lawn that surrounded the great white house in which he lived with his grandfather suddenly rose together in a flock as if hearing an inaudible signal, and disappeared into a clump of trees far off.

"There they all go," the boy told his grandfather.

"They they go," the old man repeated.

"Are you glad they're gone?" the young boy wondered.

"They're not really gone. Not South," the old man told the boy. "It isn't time yet—it's only July."

"Oh, I knowed they hadn't gone South," the boy told his grandfather. "I saw them yesterday do it. They practice like this all day long. They twitter and twitter and twitter, then they all get silent and then *zoom*, they all fly off like they knowed it was time."

"*Knew*," the grandfather corrected.

"Yes, *knew*," the boy nodded, and put his hand gently on his grandfather's hand.

"Birds are really strange creatures," the old man admitted. "They remember always where to go, where to build their nests, where to return to. . . ." He shook his head.

"They know to go South when it's cold," the boy agreed. "Except the sparrows. They stay all winter, poor little fellows. They are tough. They don't have no more feathers than the other birds, yet they stay right on, don't they?"

The grandfather nodded.

"Maybe, though, they *do* have more feathers and we can't see them," the boy added, thinking.

"That could be," the old man told his grandson, and he brought his cane up now painfully, and then pressed down with it with his hand.

The boy waited a little for his grandfather to say something more, and the old man, sensing the boy's need for words, said: "Did you like your chocolate racing car?"

"It was sweet and bitter and sweet all at the same time, and then at the very end it was soapy."

"Soapy?" the grandfather wondered.

The boy nodded.

"Well, then there was something wrong with it," the old man complained faintly.

"No," the boy said airily. "That's the way the sweet and the bitter get after you have them both together. See," he said pulling on his grandfather's cane a little, "after you taste the sweet you taste the bitter and after you taste the sweet again you taste the sweet and the bitter, and it's only soapy for a second!"

"I see," the grandfather nodded.

"And then it's all sweet!" The boy laughed, and he jumped up and down on the porch steps, making strange little sounds imitating nobody knew what.

"And I lost a tooth!" the boy told his grandfather.

"Cook told me," the old man informed him.

"Tonight when I go to bed, I am going to put it under my pillow and when I wake up in the morning do you know what is going to be under where I slept all night?"

The grandfather smiled and shook his head.

"A pot of gold," the boy told him.

"What will you do with it?" the grandfather asked.

"I might turn into a bird and go South then," the boy told him.

"But you wouldn't want to leave your old granddad and Cook," the grandfather chided.

The boy thought a moment and said, "I would fly back for supper."

"Well, it will be interesting to see your pot of gold tomorrow," the old man agreed.

"You really think I will get it then?" the boy asked.

"All wishes like that come true," the grandfather said somewhat gravely. "It's because they're a . . . a *pure* wish."

"A *pure* wish?" the boy wondered, scratching his nose. "What's that?"

"Well, like pure candy; you've had that, you know."

The boy shook his head.

"Your chocolate racing car is pure candy," the grandfather said, unsure this was so, and no conviction in his voice.

"Oh," the boy answered.

"All you really wished for, you see," the grandfather explained, "was to have your wish come true. You really hadn't thought what you would do with your wish and your pot of gold."

"Yes," the boy agreed, but his attention wandered.

"So tonight when you go to sleep you must just think that you want the pot of gold, and that is all you want. And don't wish for it too hard, you know."

"No?" the boy raised his voice.

"Not too hard. That would frighten the good fairy away."

"The good fairy?" the boy wondered.

"Yes. Who did you think brought your pot of gold?"

"I thought," the boy felt his way. "I thought . . . somebody dead."

"What?" the old man said, and he moved his cane again so that now it pointed down to the grass where the birds had gathered in a flock.

"Cook didn't really tell me who did bring it," the boy said, studying the confusion on his grandfather's face.

"Yes," the old man said absently, and then looking at his grandson he said, "well, it's really the good fairy, I expect. Don't you know about her?"

The boy shook his head.

"Well, she is the one who's supposed to bring the gold." And the old man laughed rather loudly.

"Do you believe in her?" the boy asked.

"The good fairy?" the old man said, and he began to laugh again, but stopped. "Yes, I do," he said after a pause and with a sleepy serious expression.

The grandfather fished his heavy gold watch out of his vest pocket and looked at its face.

"Seven P.M., he said.

"Seven P.M.," the boy repeated. "One hour to bedtime."

"That's right," the grandfather said, and he put his hand on the boy's head.

"Why don't you want to go South?" the young boy wondered, suddenly.

"Well," the old man stirred in his chair. "Memories, I suppose, you know." But then looking at his grandson he knew the boy did *not* know, and he said, "It's a long story."

"You don't remember why?" the boy asked.

"When you're older I will talk about it," the old man began. "You see there's so much explanation to it, and well, I'm very old, and it tires me out when I make long explanations."

"What is *explanation*—just telling everything, then?"

"Yes," the old man smiled. "And if I told you why I don't want to go South why we'd be here for days!'

"But we are anyhow!" the boy exclaimed. "We're always just standing and sitting and standing and talking here or watching the birds."

The old man was silent.

"Ain't we?" the boy said.

"Well, if I was a bird I would *never* go South," the old man spoke almost as if to himself.

The boy waited and then when his grandfather said no more he told him: "I would always come home at dark, I think, if I was a bird."

"Yes, sir, *tomorrow,*" the old man's voice sounded, taking on warmth, "you'll have your pot of gold!"

"Hurray!" the small boy shouted, and he ran around the old man's chair making sounds now that were those of a jet.

"What will you buy me tomorrow?" the boy asked his grandfather.

"But tomorrow you will have your own pot of gold!" the grandfather told his grandson. "You'll be rich!"

"Will I then?" the boy wondered.

"Don't you believe you'll have it?" the old man interrogated.

"No," the boy said softly.

"But you must believe," the grandfather warned him.

"Why?" the boy asked, looking closely into his grandfather's face.

"You must always believe in one thing, that one thing."

"What is *that one thing?*" the boy asked, an almost scared look on his face.

"Oh, it's hard to say," the old man admitted failure again.

"Not like going South now, don't tell me again," the boy complained.

"No, this is even harder to explain than going South, but I will try to tell you."

The old man drew his grandson closer to him and arranged the collar of the boy's shirt. He said: "There is always one thing a person believes and wants to believe even if he doesn't believe it."

"Ahem," the boy said, standing on only one leg.

"Do you see?" the old man asked, his face soft and smiling.

"Yes," the boy replied, his voice hard.

"All right, then," the old man went on. "There is this one thing you want and you want it more than anything in the world. You see?"

"Like the birds knowing where to fly, you mean?" the boy was cautious.

"Yes," the old man doubted this, and then said, "but more like your pot of gold."

"Oh," the boy replied.

"You want this one thing, and you have to go on believing in it, no matter what."

"Well, what is the thing?" the boy smiled broadly now, showing the place in his mouth where he had lost his tooth, which was a front one.

"Only the person who knows can tell!" the grandfather said loudly as though this were a joke now.

"But am I old enough to know?" the boy said, puzzled and surprised.

"You're old enough and you should tell me now," the grandfather encouraged him.

"So," the boy paused, screwing his eyes shut, and he stood first on one foot and then on another. "I would like my father and mother both to be alive again, and all of us, including you, living South."

The old man opened his mouth and closed it again.

"Isn't that the right answer?" the boy said, worried.

"Yes, of course," the old man hurriedly agreed.

"You don't act like it was the right answer," the boy complained.

"Well, it is, anyhow. The only thing was—I was thinking about wishes that are about the future, you see."

"Oh," the boy was disappointed. Then in a kind of querulous voice he said, "My wish wasn't the future?"

"It's so hard to explain," the grandfather laughed, and he roughed up the boy's hair.

"Well," the boy said, "let's talk about things we can tell each other."

The grandfather laughed.

The light was beginning to die slowly in the trees, and a full rounded moon began to show in the near distance.

Suddenly the boy said *Oh* in a scared voice.

"What is it?" the grandfather was concerned.

"I think I lost my tooth," the boy said.

"You did?" the grandfather was even more alarmed now than the boy.

"I did, I lost it." He felt suddenly in his pockets.

"When we were talking about the birds, you know, I throwed my hand out . . . and the tooth must have been in my hand."

"You *threw* your hand out. Well, then it's in the grass," the grandfather said.

"Yes," the boy agreed.

The old man got out of his chair and his grandson helped him silently down the twelve steps that led to the long walk about which extended the immense lawn where the tooth had been thrown.

They searched patiently in the long grass, which had needed cutting for some time.

"It was such a little tooth," the boy said, as though he realized this fact for the first time.

The old man could not bend over very far, but his eyes, which were still keen, looked sharply about him for the tooth.

"Oh, what shall I ever do!" the boy said suddenly.

"But it will turn up!" the old man cried, but there was the same note of disappointment and fear in his voice, which, communicating itself to the boy, caused the latter to weep.

"You mustn't cry," the grandfather was stern. "It won't do at all!"

"But the pot of gold and all!" the boy cried.

"It doesn't matter at all," the grandfather said, and he touched the boy on the face.

"But you told me it did," the boy wept now.

"I told you *what?*" the old man said.

"You told me there was just that one thing you should want to believe in."

"But you've only lost your tooth," the old man replied. "And we'll find it. It isn't lost forever. The gardener will find it when he comes."

"Oh, I'm afraid not," the boy said, wandering about now picking up the grass by the handfuls, looking and watching about him in the fading light.

"If we only hadn't let Cook take the flashlight we might locate it with that," the grandfather said, a few minutes later, when the light was quite gone.

The boy now just stood in one place staring down at the grass.

"I think we'll have to give up the search for tonight," the grandfather finally said.

"But this is the only night I can have my wish!" the boy cried "This is the ONLY night."

"Nonsense," the grandfather told him. "Not true at all."

"But it is, it is," the boy contradicted his grandfather, gravely.

"How do you know?" the grandfather wondered.

"My mother told me," the boy said.

"But you don't . . . you don't remember her!" the grandfather stared into the growing dark.

"She told me in my sleep," the boy said, his voice plain, unemphatic.

The grandfather looked at his grandson's face but the dark hid it and its expression from him.

"Let's go up the steps now," the grandfather told him.

The small boy helped the old man up the twelve steps, and at the last one the old man laughed, making fun of his fatigue.

"Don't ever get old now, don't you ever do that," he laughed.

The grandfather sat down heavily in the chair, his cane thrown out as though commanding something, or somebody.

"We'll find your tooth tomorrow, or we'll all be hanged," the grandfather said cheerily. "And we won't let Cook take our flashlight again, will we?"

The boy did not answer. He stood as he stood every night beside his grandfather, looking out over the western sky, tonight half-seeing the red harvest moon rise.

"I will buy you something different tomorrow," the grandfather said, "so that it will be a real surprise. Do you hear?"

The boy said yes.

"You're not crying now," the grandfather said. "That's good."

The boy nodded.

"I'm glad you're brave too, because a boy should not cry, really, no matter even. . . . Well, he should never cry."

"But I don't know what to believe in now," the boy said in a dry old voice.

"Fiddlesticks," the old man said. "Now come over here and sit on my lap and I will talk to you some more."

The boy moved slowly and sat down on his grandfather's lap.

"Ouch," the grandfather said playfully when he felt how heavy the boy was.

"Just the two of us," the old man said. "Just the two of us here, but we're good friends, aren't we. Good, good old friends."

He pushed the boy's head tight against his breast so he

would not hear the sounds that came out now like a confused and trackless torrent, making ridiculous the quiet of evening, and he closed his own eyes so that he would not see the moon.

About Jessie Mae

"I don't visit Jessie Mae's any more because of her untidiness," Myrtle said to Mrs. Hemlock as the two women walked through the garden, where they had been talking, toward Mrs. Hemlock's kitchen, where Myrtle was going to copy down a special recipe for the older woman.

"But I didn't know it had gone so far," Mrs. Hemlock said with mild unbelief.

"I didn't say it had gone *too* far now," Myrtle told her. "Nothing is under any order or control, that's all."

"And that I can believe," Mrs. Hemlock agreed.

"You see, Jessie Mae's never had to do anything for herself," Myrtle explained.

Mrs. Hemlock stared at her friend's youthful face, in the late morning Florida light, the desire for *more* written on her own expectant mouth and heavy double chin.

"You know Jessie Mae was *twice* an heiress," and Myrtle hit the word as hard as possible in order to begin at the beginning of her knowledge.

"I knew she had everything, of course," Mrs. Hemlock said in somewhat hushed tones now, as though a matter of

considerable delicacy had been disclosed. She looked down
at her apron suddenly and removed a long ravelling which
had come to rest there.

Myrtle looked quickly at Mrs. Hemlock's apron and
said, "That's cunning."

"It's Portuguese or Spanish or something," Mrs. Hemlock smiled, opening the back screen to her kitchen.

"You know, you have beautiful things, Mrs. Hemlock,"
Myrtle said.

Mrs. Hemlock laughed pleasantly.

"I love to come to *your* house," Myrtle told her.

"But I can't understand Jessie Mae's being that *untidy*,"
Mrs. Hemlock seemed very surprised, and she pointed
quickly to a large easy chair which she had brought into
her kitchen specially for her many visitors. Myrtle sat down
with a great sigh of pleasure.

"This chair!" Myrtle groaned loudly and pretended to
collapse from their long earlier talk in the garden.

Mrs. Hemlock smiled at this compliment, too, and
chuckled mildly, her double chin moving slightly as if she
were singing a lullaby.

"I'm Jessie Mae's distant cousin, you know," Myrtle
said suddenly.

Mrs. Hemlock paused a second because she was not sure
she knew this or not. But dimly, from many years back
in certain St. Augustine circles, a faint recollection stirred
in her brain.

"I remember," Mrs. Hemlock nodded, and opening the
refrigerator she moved swiftly for such a stout woman to
hand Myrtle a tall cool glass of fruit punch, thickly frosted,
and non-alcoholic.

"You jewel!" Myrtle almost squealed. "You think of
everything. And you *have* everything."

Mrs. Hemlock could not conceal her pleasure again. Her heavy, healthy face flushed slightly from the additional praise.

"I'm alone and I have to keep busy at something," Mrs. Hemlock glanced at her kitchen.

"But most women wouldn't bother," Myrtle said. "You're *always* cooking. And so generous in sending around things to we neighbors. Why you're making us all fat, too!" Myrtle laughed loudly.

Mrs. Hemlock started at this, but then she laughed pleasantly also.

"I suppose eating is a sin," Mrs. Hemlock pretended seriousness.

"Nothing that gives one pleasure like this is," Myrtle was firm on this point, and Mrs. Hemlock could see Myrtle was thinking of Jessie Mae again.

"Well!" Mrs. Hemlock exclaimed, drinking now some of her own fruit punch and hoping Myrtle would go back to her first subject, "It's nice we're all a bit different."

"It's wonderful," Myrtle said, referring to the drink. "And I suppose it's a secret recipe . . ."

"No, no," Mrs. Hemlock deprecated this, but acted abstracted now, almost as if tasting something in the drink which she had not remembered putting there. Then suddenly she broke out: "I didn't know, as a matter of fact, you *were* Jessie Mae's distant cousin."

Myrtle put down her glass of juice on the kitchen table, which was provided with a handsome imported linen table cloth, fresh and spotless.

"I really had forgotten, that is," Mrs. Hemlock said in a kind of apology.

"I'm really one of the last of her own people," Myrtle spoke indifferently, but with a certain tone which implied that the relationship might be important for others to remember.

"Jessie Mae is of course basically a fine person," Mrs. Hemlock stated, fearful now that she had perhaps stressed the untidiness too much, even though Myrtle had brought the whole subject up in the garden.

"Mrs. Hemlock, Jessie Mae's in terrible shape!" Myrtle suddenly changed any direction toward or need for apology, and she stared at her drink as if she had promised herself not to touch it again.

Mrs. Hemlock moistened her lips critically, as if she, too, did not require the refreshment now of the punch.

"Is Jessie Mae *worried* or something?" Mrs. Hemlock felt her way in the break which had come into the conversation.

"Worried, my foot," Myrtle sprang suddenly at this suggestion, and she picked up her glass again and tasted the punch.

"She lives to worry other people, if you want to know. . . . Or if you really think about it, too much money and not enough to do . . . Do you know she has a maid to *dress* her now!"

Mrs. Hemlock's heavy face was suffused with the flush of pleasure. And although she had stood until now in her professional guise as hostess, she decided to sit down. She sat directly in front of Myrtle and said: "She *doesn't!*"

Myrtle looked almost cross at Mrs. Hemlock, for she felt the latter's exclamation was hardly necessary even in a rhetorical sense.

"I don't think Jessie Mae does a thing for herself any more," Myrtle was definite on this. "She has, you know, eight servants."

"And yet her house remains so—" and Mrs. Hemlock

was going to describe the untidiness again but Myrtle had already gone ahead with:

"Jessie Mae orders everything there is to be done. And you can bet your bottom dollar that if there's untidiness she orders that too!"

Mrs. Hemlock gasped quietly and lowered her head as if to take in all the meaning of the statement, but Myrtle did not see fit to let her contemplate anything at that moment.

"She keeps these eight servants busy, let me tell you. For every one of the rooms in her house, and there must be twenty if there's one—they're all in *use!*"

Mrs. Hemlock's eyes came open wide and then closed, and her mouth closed hard too like one who had found more put in it than she had been ready for.

"That's only the beginning!" Myrtle cried.

Mrs. Hemlock's eyes came open now and there was such a look of perfect satisfaction on her face that Myrtle's own expression softened and glowed with the reflected pleasure from her older friend.

"You *don't* know about her!" Myrtle intoned with happiness, sure at last of Mrs. Hemlock's ignorance.

"I was only at her house in the old days, when she entertained General Waite so much," Mrs. Hemlock said, coolly matter-of-fact, a hint of total abdication in her tone. "Jessie Mae's brother was more or less head of the house then."

"Well, Corliss liked to act like he was," Myrtle took this statement up. "But Jessie Mae was running the whole place even then, and running him too. He died of her bossing, many people think."

"Then, of course, I've been there several times to tea, and to her art fairs," Mrs. Hemlock put in rather firmly before stepping down altogether.

"Oh those are nothing, my dear, I'm sorry to say. You see you have to spend the night to know how it really is!" Myrtle was suddenly indignant now, but Mrs. Hemlock could see that her indignation was over the principle of Jessie Mae's behavior.

For just a second Mrs. Hemlock looked at her large red recipe book lying open to the place where Myrtle was to fill in the instructions for baking Bavarian cookies. But then she moved her eyes away from the book back directly into Myrtle's face. She wanted Myrtle to know now that she didn't know anything about Jessie Mae, and that she wanted more than anything else to find out all there was.

Myrtle saw this expression on Mrs. Hemlock's face, and put her hands in her lap as a signal they could begin in earnest.

"Jessie Mae's trouble is she won't have anything planned or in order, until she wants it. And she doesn't know what she wants until the moment she does want it!"

Myrtle suddenly stopped there like one who has not quite caught the meaning of her own words. Mrs. Hemlock stared at her and her mouth came open again, and it was this open-mouthed expression and the immense interest on Mrs. Hemlock's face, together with the wonderful health and cleanliness of the latter, and the wonderful comfort and luxury of her kitchen that made Myrtle want to stay on here, perhaps indefinitely. She did not know when things had been better for a talk.

"More punch?" Mrs. Hemlock said in her most encouraging tone.

"I'd love more!"

"And some of my ice box fudge bars with it!" Mrs. Hemlock coaxed, almost a bit hysterical with the pleasure which the Jessie Mae story was giving her.

"I'd love some fudge bars too," Myrtle said, absentmindedly, still hesitating, it was obvious, whether to give all she knew about their common acquaintance now, or perhaps hold some last bit still back, for another time, or forever.

"As I say," Mrs. Hemlock spoke in her matter-of-fact voice, afraid whatever she said would spoil the "more" that might come, "as I say, I was never a *friend* of Jessie Mae's, but I've known her for twenty-five years."

Myrtle did not even consider this but thanked Mrs. Hemlock for the fudge bars and the second glass of punch.

"I could eat these all day," Myrtle said chewing softly, not to be hurried or budged. She made a sound of pleasure.

"I wonder you don't win prizes with your culinary genius, Mrs. Hemlock," Myrtle purred, deliberating. "You should be famous."

The older woman bowed her head in pleasure and the blush of her health and good living covered her face and throat.

But both women waited for the signal to begin again, calmly now, but with tremendous expectation.

"I know everything about her," Myrtle said suddenly.

One would not have known Mrs. Hemlock had broken their talk by going to the icebox for the fudge bars. It was almost as though Jessie Mae herself were there before them on the TV screen, helpless and exposed for all their comments.

"I lived with her for a month!" Myrtle said after she had quit chewing on the fudge bars. "In 1952!"

Mrs. Hemlock waited.

"A month, mind you!"

"Then of course you do know," Mrs. Hemlock said in a voice close to awe.

"I was afraid every minute," Myrtle said.

Mrs. Hemlock showed a slight lack of comprehension.

"You spoke of her untidiness, Mrs. Hemlock," Myrtle swept on. "Well," she laughed, "you wouldn't think that that was largely connected with her leaving her jewels everywhere. She left thousands and thousands of dollars worth of diamonds in my room."

Mrs. Hemlock shook her head.

"Then one evening I discovered in the top bureau drawer of my room enough other jewels for the Queen herself!"

Mrs. Hemlock began to say something but Myrtle hardly paused long enough to allow her friend to tense her mouth.

"I couldn't stand that kind of untidiness, if you please, and besides I'm not so sure her untidiness, as we call it, wasn't purposeful."

"Well!" Mrs. Hemlock managed to cry.

"It's part of her way of getting even!"

"But what would she want to get even for when she's got everything!" Mrs. Hemlock propelled the question into the room and beyond into the garden.

"You don't know everything," Myrtle cautioned again. "She hates men, she hates women even more. And she's not only untidy. You started to use the right word when we were outside. She's *dirty!*"

Mrs. Hemlock let out a moan of weak remonstrance.

"I could tell you things," Myrtle said, "but we're here in a beautiful tidy house with such wonderful things to eat. I won't."

Myrtle had suddenly stopped talking, and she lay back in her chair, leaving Mrs. Hemlock with a look of complete and unexpected emptiness on her red face.

Then, perhaps of a second mind, Myrtle said: "Her whole life is to get back at everybody. Hence the servants. Hence the parties at which nothing is quite right. Hence the jewels strewn everywhere to make everybody feel they are suspected of stealing. Who wants to go to a house where jewels are strewn everywhere. Why it makes the closest of us to her wince! And don't think she doesn't accuse people of taking them. And not just the servants!"

"Why, she sounds . . . *gone*," Mrs. Hemlock had groped for the word but did not look satisfied when she had got it.

"No," Myrtle corrected politely, smiling quickly, "Jessie Mae is just hateful . . . She's not *gone* as you say. A man, a strong old-fashioned type over her would have gone a long way to getting the house tidied up and the jewels either sold or put in a vault. But she's never had a strong hand over her, and since the day her old father died, she's done just as she pleased every second . . ."

"Really, I never!" Mrs. Hemlock began.

"But the thing nobody seems to know," Myrtle said, sitting up still more straight, and her face a peculiar shade, "and the thing nobody can believe even when you tell them is that the whole house is nothing but an excuse for dogs!"

Mrs. Hemlock's chin trembled but she said nothing.

"Jessie Mae has thirty pedigreed dogs in those rooms upstairs if she has one!"

Mrs. Hemlock closed her eyes again, but she could not conceal the pleasure that rested on her mouth and chin.

Myrtle waited until her friend opened her eyes and then she said: "Jessie Mae sleeps downstairs, where she made her brother sleep before her. The dogs live upstairs, and there's a servant on duty for every room of them."

"You're funning!" Mrs. Hemlock used an old word and an old tone that sounded like *Amen*.

"And when I stayed there that month," Myrtle said,

her mouth dry from the exertion, "she let me see the whole performance, since I had to sleep downstairs with her in any case. After all the visitors and the bores had left, she let the dogs out of their upstairs rooms, and then they would romp and tear and romp and tear, and that old woman ran and romped right along with them, laughing and shouting at them, and the dogs all yelping and carrying on like a pack of wild animals after her until you wouldn't know which acted the nuttier, she or the dogs."

"Good God!" Mrs. Hemlock turned a deep orange now, and she fanned her face with her fat hand.

"I usually never talk about Jessie Mae to anybody," Myrtle intoned.

"Of course," Mrs. Hemlock nodded, a tone of firm moral philosophy in her voice.

"But you've been so kind and considerate, to all of we neighbors," Myrtle almost scolded, "and especially to me, that I think of you, Mrs. Hemlock, as a confidante."

"Thank you, Myrtle. I'm touched," Mrs. Hemlock managed to get out.

"It's the truth. You've been an angel. Why you've baked for us and sent us things. This could be another Delmonico's!" she waved with her hand. "I've never tasted such cooking. And the comparison between your wonderful generosity and neatness and normal ways always comes as such a distinct contrast with Jessie Mae, who is, after all, my cousin, but who never does anything for anybody, and who just isn't anyhow the kind of person you want to visit."

Myrtle stopped, perhaps in realization she had told more than she had ever known she knew.

"But the poor old thing," Mrs. Hemlock ventured.

"Well, with all her wealth why doesn't she try to

straighten herself out, for pity's sake. She could help so many people if she cared about anybody but herself."

Myrtle waited now finally for Mrs. Hemlock to speak, but the older woman sat there quietly, a fudge bar still untasted in her hand, thinking about Jesse Mae's running up and down with the dogs.

"I'm not surprised now the house looked so bad," Mrs. Hemlock said at last, but with a kind of dreamy expression that lacked conviction.

Myrtle was so tired she just lay back in the chair.

"Would you like a nice home-made devilled ham sandwich with a good cup of strong coffee?" Mrs. Hemlock said invitingly. "You look *awfully* tired, Myrtle."

"Why, I'd love one, of course . . . But shouldn't I fill in that recipe for you first," Myrtle said, and she took out of her apron pocket a piece of paper which contained her directions for baking Bavarian cookies.

"I think you deserve a sandwich first. Copying is awfully tiring too."

"Well, you know me and your cooking," Myrtle giggled.

"Why, I would have *never* known that about Jessie Mae if you hadn't just happened to be walking through the garden today," Mrs. Hemlock said, and she began to boil the water for the coffee.

"I know you won't tell anybody," Myrtle said. "Because as you know, she *is* part of my family, though you'd never know it the way she acts."

"I understand, of course," and Mrs. Hemlock smiled from above her pink chin. "But it *does* explain at last the . . . *untidiness*. My stars, yes."

Mrs. Hemlock was firm on that point.

Myrtle nodded abstractedly and both women were silent now waiting for the coffee to be ready.

The Lesson

"This is not lady's day at the pool," Mr. Diehl said. "I can't admit her."

"But she pleaded so."

Mr. Diehl was about to give his lesson to a young man and wanted no women in the pool. He knew that if a woman entered the pool during the lesson she would distract the young man, who was already nervous about learning to swim. The young man was quite upset already, as he was going to have to go to a country house where there was lots of swimming and boating, and if he didn't know how, his hosts would be very put out with him. They might never invite him again. At any rate that was his story, and besides, he was the commander's son.

"But my grandmother always wants as many people to come into the pool as possible," the girl said. Her grandmother owned the pool.

"I have worked for your grandmother for a long time," Mr. Diehl, the swimming instructor said, "and I'm sure that she would not want a woman in the pool at this hour who does not belong to the club and so far as I know doesn't even know how to swim."

"Well, I asked her that," the girl said.

"And what did she say?" the swimming instructor wanted to know.

"She said she could swim."

"Just the same she can wait until the lesson is over. It takes only half an hour."

"I told her that, but she wanted to go in the pool right away. She has gone downstairs to change."

"For Christ's sake," Mr. Diehl said.

His pupil, the commander's son, was already splashing around in the shallow water, waiting for the lesson.

"Go and tell her in a half hour."

The girl looked as though she was not going to tell the woman.

"If your grandmother were here she would back me up on this," Mr. Diehl said.

"But she's not here and my instructions were to do as best I thought."

"As best you thought," Mr. Diehl considered this, looking at the girl. She was sixteen, but he knew she had a slow mind and he wondered what had ever made Mrs. Schuck leave the pool in the hands of such an immature person.

"Look," Mr. Diehl said. "Just go and tell the woman that I can't have her in the pool while I am giving this special lesson."

"Well, I can't forbid her the pool very well, now, can I. If she wants to come in! This club isn't that exclusive and she knows one of the members."

"I don't care if she knows the man who invented swimming, she can't come in. Is that clear?"

"Mr. Diehl, you forget that I am the granddaughter of the owner of the pool."

"I am responsible for what goes on in the water, am I not?"

"Yes, I'll go along with you there."

"All right then," Mr. Diehl said, as though having made his point. "Go tell her I can't have her in the water until after the lesson. Can't you do that?"

"No," the girl said. "I can't tell that to a perfectly good customer."

"You have this pool mixed up with a public dance hall or something. This is not exactly a money-making organization, as your grandmother must have told you. It is a club. Not open to everybody. And this unknown woman should not have been allowed in here anyhow. Not at all."

"I know better," the girl said. "Many nice people come here just for an occasional swim."

"Not unless they are known," Mr. Diehl said.

"But she knows a member," the girl pointed out.

"Who is the member?" Mr. Diehl wanted to know.

"Oh, I can't remember," the girl told him.

"But I know every member by name," Mr. Diehl was insistent. "I've been swimming instructor here now for nine years."

"I know, I know," the girl said. "But this woman has every right to come in here."

"She's not coming in the water."

"Well, I don't know what to tell her. She's already putting on her suit."

"Then she can take it right off again," Mr. Diehl said.

"But not here, though," the girl tried a joke. Mr. Diehl did not laugh.

"What I'm trying to get you to see, Polly," Mr. Diehl said, and it was the first time he had ever called her by name, "is that this is a pretty high-class place. Do you know by chance who that boy is who is waiting for the lesson."

Mr. Diehl waited for the girl to answer.

"I don't know who he is," she replied.

"That is Commander Jackson's son."

"And he doesn't know how to swim?"

"What has that got to do with it?" the swimming instructor said.

"Well, I'm surprised is all."

"Look, time is slipping away. I don't want to have any more argument with you, Polly. But I'm sure your grandmother would back me up on this all the way if she were here. Is there any way we can reach her by telephone?"

"I have no idea where she went."

"Well, this strange woman cannot come into the pool now."

"I am not going down to the locker room and tell her to put her clothes back on, so there," Polly said.

She was very angry, but she had also gotten a little scared.

"Then I'm going to have to tell your grandmother how nasty you've been."

"How nasty *I've* been?"

Mr. Diehl went up to the girl and put his hands on her shoulder as he often did to his students. "Look here now," he said. He did not realize how he was affecting the girl and how the water fell from him on her blouse. She looked at his biceps as they moved almost over her mouth and the way his chest rose and fell. She had always lowered her eyes when she met him in the hall, avoiding the sight of his wet, dripping quality, the many keys held in his hand, his whistle for the days when they practiced champion swimming. He had seemed to her like something that should always remain splashing about and breathing heavily in water.

"Polly, will you please cooperate with me," Mr. Diehl said.

"I don't think I can," she said.

He put down his arms in a gesture of despair. "Will you please, please just this once go down to the ladies' dressing room and tell that woman that you've made a mistake and that she can't come into the pool just now?"

Polly looked out now into the water where the commander's son was floating around by holding on to a rubber tire.

"I just can't tell her," Polly said, turning red.

"You can't tell her," Mr. Diehl observed. Then: "Look, do you know who the commander is?"

"Well, doesn't everybody?" Polly answered.

"Do you know or don't you?" Mr. Diehl wanted to know. Some more water fell from him as he gesticulated, wetting her blouse and her arms a little, and she was sure that water continued to fall from him no matter how long he had been out of the pool. She could hear him breathing and she could not help noticing his chest rise and fall as though he were doing a special swimming feat just for her in this room.

"Polly!" he said.

"I can't! I can't!" she cried.

He could see now that there was something else here, perhaps fear of something, he could not tell, he did not want to know.

"You're not going to run into any difficulty in just telling her, are you, that you didn't know the rules and that she will have to wait until the lesson is over."

"I can't and I won't," Polly said, and she refused to look at him.

The commander's son was watching them from the middle of the shallow part of the pool, but he did not act as though he was impatient for the lesson to begin, and Polly remembered what a severe instructor Mr. Diehl was said to be. Sometimes while she had sat outside in the reception room she had heard Mr. Diehl shout all the way from the pool.

"Look, do we have to go all over this again?" Mr. Diehl said. "You know the commander."

"I know the commander, of course," she said.

"Do you know he is the most influential member of the club here?"

Polly did not say anything.

"He built this pool, Polly. Not your grandmother. Did you know that?"

She felt that she might weep now, so she did not say anything.

"Are you hearing me?" Mr. Diehl wanted to know.

"*Hearing* you!" she cried, distracted.

"All right now," he said, and he put his hand on her again and she thought some more drops of water fell from him.

"I can't see how anybody would know," she said. "How would the commander know if a young woman went into his pool. And what would his son out there care."

"His son doesn't like people in the pool when he is taking a lesson," Mr. Diehl explained. "He wants it strictly private, and the commander wants it that way too."

"And the commander pays you to want it that way also."

"Polly, I'm trying to be patient."

"I'm not going to tell her she can't come in," Polly said.

She stood nearer now to the edge of the pool away from his moving arms and chest and the dripping water that she felt still came off them.

"Step away from the edge, please, Polly," he said, and he took hold of her arm drawing her firmly over to him, in his old manner with special pupils when he was about to impart to them some special secret of swimming.

"Don't always touch me," she said, but so faintly that it was hardly a reproach.

"Polly, listen to me," Mr. Diehl was saying to her. "I've known you since you were a little girl. Right?"

"Known me?" Polly said, and she felt the words only come vaguely toward her now.

"Been a friend of your family, haven't I, for a good long time. Your grandmother knew me when I was only a boy. She paid for some of my tuition in college."

"College," Polly nodded to the last word she had heard, so that he would think she was listening.

"You'll feel all right about this, Polly, and you will, I know, help me now that I've explained it to you."

"No, I can't," she said, awake again.

"You can't what?" Mr. Diehl said.

"I can't is all," she said but she spoke, as she herself recognized, like a girl talking in her sleep.

The hothouse heat of the swimming pool and the close presence of Mr. Diehl, a man she had always instinctively avoided, had made her forget in a sense why they were standing here before the water. Somewhere in a dressing room, she remembered, there was a woman who in a little while was going to do something wrong that would displease Mr. Diehl, and suddenly she felt glad this was so.

"Mr. Diehl, I am going," she said, but she made no motion to leave, and he knew from her words that she was not going. They were going on talking, he knew. It was like his students, some of them said they could never be champions, but they always were. He made them so. Some of the timid ones said they could never swim, the water was terror to them, but they always did swim. Mr. Diehl had never known failure with anything. He never said this but he showed it.

"Now you listen to me," Mr. Diehl said. "All you have to do is go and tell her. She can sit outside with you and watch television."

"The set isn't working," Polly said, and she walked over close to the edge of the pool.

"Please come over here now," Mr. Diehl said, and he took hold of her and brought her over to where he had been standing. "Polly, I would never have believed this of you."

"Believed what?" she said, and her mind could not remember now again why exactly they were together here. She kept looking around as though perhaps she had duties she had forgotten somewhere. Then as she felt more and more unlike herself, she put her hand on Mr. Diehl's arm.

"Believed," he was saying, and she saw his white teeth near her as though the explanation of everything were in the teeth themselves—"believed you would act so incorrigible. So bad, Polly. Yes, that's the word. Bad."

"Incorrigible," she repeated, and she wondered what exactly that had always meant. It was a word that had passed before her eyes a few times but nobody had ever pronounced it to her.

"I would never want your grandmother to even know we have had to have this long argument. I will never tell her."

"I will never tell her," Polly said, expressionless, drowsily echoing his words.

"Thank you, Polly, and of course I didn't mean to tell you you didn't have to. But listen to me."

She put her hand now very heavily on his arm and leaned there.

"Are you all right, Polly," he said, and she realized suddenly that it was the first time he had every really been aware of her being anything at all, and now when it was too late, when she felt too bad to even tell him, he had begun to grow aware.

"Polly," he said.

"Yes, Mr. Diehl," she answered and suddenly he looked down at her hand on his arm, it was pressing there, and he had become, of course, conscious of it.

He did not know what to do, she realized, and ill as she felt, the pleasure of having made him uncomfortable soothed her. She knew she was going to be very ill, but she had had at least, then, this triumph, the champion was also uncomfortable.

"You'll go and tell her then," Mr. Diehl said, but she knew now that he was not thinking about the woman anymore. The woman, the lesson, the pool had all lost their meaning and importance now.

"Polly," he said.

"I will tell her," she managed to say, still holding him tight.

"Polly, what is it?" he exclaimed.

He took her arm off him roughly, and his eyes moved about the room as though he were looking for somebody to help. His eyes fell cursorily upon the commander's son, and then back to her, but it was already too late, she had begun to topple toward him, her hands closed over his arms, and her head went pushing into his chest, rushing him with a strength he had seldom felt before.

When they fell into the water it was very difficult for him to get hold of her at all. She had swallowed so much water, and she had struck at him so hard, and had said words all the time nobody could have understood or believed but him. It was her speaking and struggling, as he said later, which had caused her to swallow so much water.

He had had to give her partial artificial respiration, a thing he had not done really in all his life, although he had taken all the courses in it as befitted a champion swimmer.

"Get out of the pool for God's sake and call somebody," Mr. Diehl yelled to the commander's son, and the boy left off hanging to the rubber tire, and slowly began to climb out of the shallow water.

"Get some speed on there, for Christ's sake," he said.

"Yes, sir," the commander's son replied.

"I can't be responsible for this whole goddam thing," he shouted after the retreating boy.

"Now see here, Polly, for Christ's sake," Mr. Diehl began looking down at her.

She opened her eyes and looked at him.

"You certainly pulled one over me!" he cried looking at her, rage and fear on his mouth.

She lay there watching his chest move, feeling the drops of water falling over her from his body, and smelling behind the strong chemical odor of the pool the strong smell that must be Mr. Diehl himself, the champion.

"I'll go tell her now," Polly said.

Mr. Diehl stared at her.

"She must never come here at all," Polly said. "I think I see that now."

Mr. Diehl stretched out his hand to her to lift her up.

"Go away, please," she said. "Don't lean over me, please, and let the water fall from you on me. Please, please go back into the pool. I don't want you close now. Go back into the pool."

Encore

"He's in that Greek restaurant every night. I thought you knew that," Merta told her brother.

"What does he do in it?" Spence said, wearily attentive.

"I don't go to Greek restaurants and I don't spy on him," she said.

"Then how do you know so certainly he is there every night?"

"How do you know anything? He's not popular at the college. He says he likes to talk to Spyro, the restaurant owner's son, about painting. I don't know what they do!"

"Well, don't tell me if you don't know," her brother said. He got up and took his hat to go.

"Of course," she continued, anxiously stepping in front of him to detain his going, "it isn't so much that Spyro is all at fault, you know. There are things wrong with Gibbs, too. As I said, he's not popular at the college. He wasn't asked to join a fraternity, you know. And the restaurant has made up for that, I suppose. It's always open for him day or night."

"Maybe you should make your own home more of a

46

place he could bring his friends to," Spence said, a kind of cold expressionless tone in his voice.

"You would say that," she repeated almost without emotion. "I don't suppose you ever half considered what it is, I mean this home. It's not a home. It's a flat, and I'm a woman without a husband."

"I know, I know, Merta. You've done it all alone. Nobody's lifted a finger but you." His weariness itself seemed to collapse when he said this, and he looked at her with genuine feeling.

"I'm not trying to get your pity. I wanted to tell somebody what was going on at Spyro's is all. I needed to talk to somebody."

"I think Spyro's is the best place he could go," Spence said.

"And Spyro's awful father and grandfather!" she cried as though seeing something from far back of dread and ugliness.

"The Matsoukases?" Spence was surprised at her vehemence.

"Yes, the Matsoukases! With their immense eyes and black beards. Old Mr. Matsoukas, the grandfather, came here one evening, and tried to get fresh with me."

"I can hardly believe it," Spence said.

"You mean I am making it up," she accused him.

"No, no, I just can't visualize it."

"And now," she returned to the only subject which interested her, "Gibbs is there all the time as though it was his home."

"Do you talk to him about it, Merta?"

"I can't. I can't tell him and nag him about not going to the Greek restaurant at night. It's glamor and life to

him, I suppose, and I suppose it *is* different. A different
sort of place. The old man hasn't allowed them to put in
juke boxes or television or anything, and you know Gibbs
likes anything funny or different, and there isn't anything
funny or different but maybe Spyro's. None of the college
crowd goes there, and Gibbs feels he's safe there from their
criticism and can drink his coffee in peace."

"Well it sounds so dull, drinking coffee in a seedy Greek
restaurant, I don't see why a mother should worry about
her son going there. And call me out of bed to talk about
it!"

"Oh Spence," she said urgently again, "he shouldn't go
there. Don't you see? He shouldn't be there."

"I don't see that at all," Spence said. "And, Merta, I
wish you would quit calling me up at this hour of the
night to talk about your son, who is nearly a grown man
by now. After all I have my profession to worry about
too. . . ."

She stared at him.

"I had to talk with somebody about Spyro," she said.

"Oh, it's Spyro then you wanted to talk about," Spence
said, the irritation growing in his manner.

"Spyro," she said vaguely, as though it were Spence who
himself had mentioned him and thus brought him to
mind. "I never cared much for that young man."

"Why not?" Spence was swift to hold her to anything
vague and indirect because he felt that vagueness and
indirectness was her method.

"Well, Spyro does all those paintings and drawings that
are so bizarre."

"Bizarre," he paused on the word. "They're nearly *good,*
if you ask me."

"I don't like Spyro," she said.

"Why don't you invite him here, if your son likes him?" he put the whole matter in her hands.

"When I work in a factory all day long, Spence...."

"You don't feel like doing anything but working in a factory," he said irritably.

"I thought my own brother would be a little more understanding," she said coldly angry.

"I wish you would be of Gibbs," he told her.

"Oh Spence, please, please."

"Please, nothing. You always have a problem, but the problem is you, Merta. You're old and tired and complaining, and because you can't put your finger on what's wrong you've decided that there's something wrong with your son because he goes, of all places, to a Greek restaurant and talks to Spyro who draws rather well and who is now making a portrait of your son."

"Spence! Don't tell me that!"

"You dear old fool, Merta," he said and he put on his hat now, which she looked at, he thought, rather critically and also with a certain envy.

"That's a nice hat," she forced herself to say at last.

"Well a doctor can't look like a nobody," he said, and then winced at his own words.

"What you should do, Merta," he hurried on with another speech, "is get some sort of hobby, become a lady bowler, get on the old women's curling team, or meet up with some gent your own age. And let your son go his own way."

"You are comforting," Merta said, pretending to find humor in his words.

"Was that Spence leaving just now?" Gibbs said, putting down some books.

Merta held her face up to be kissed by him, which he did in a manner resembling someone surreptitiously spitting out a seed.

"And how was Spyro tonight?" she said in a booming encouraging voice whose suddenness and loudness perhaps surprised even her.

He looked at her much as he had when as a small boy she had suddenly burst into the front room and asked him what he was being so very still for.

"Spyro is doing a portrait of me," he told her.

"A portrait," Merta said, trying hard to keep the disapproval out of her voice.

"That's what it is," Gibbs said, sitting down at the far end of the room and taking out his harmonica.

She closed her eyes in displeasure, but said nothing as he played "How High the Moon." He always played, it seemed, when she wanted to talk to him.

"Would you like Spyro to come to visit us some day?" she said.

"Visit us?"

"Pay a call," she smiled, closing her eyes.

"What would he pay us a call for?" he wondered. Seeing her pained hurt look, he expanded: "I mean what would he get to see here."

"Oh me," she replied laughing. "I'm so beautiful."

"Spyro thinks you don't like him," Gibbs said, and while she was saying *Tommyrot!* Gibbs went on: "In fact, he thinks everybody in this town dislikes him."

"They *are* the only Greeks, it's true," Merta said.

"And we're such a front family in town, of course!" he said with sudden fire.

"Well, your Uncle Spence is somebody," she began,

white, and her mouth gaping a little, but Gibbs started to play on the harmonica again, cutting her off.

She tried to control her feelings tonight, partly because she had such a splitting headache.

"Would you like a dish of strawberry jello?" Merta said above the sound of the harmonica playing.

"What?" he cried.

"Some strawberry jello," she repeated, a little embarrassment now in her voice.

"What would I want that for?" he asked, putting down the harmonica with impatience.

"I suddenly got hungry for some, and went out there and made it. It's set by now and ready to eat."

There was such a look of total defeat on her old gray face that Gibbs said he would have some.

"I've some fresh coffee too," she said, a touch of sophistication in her voice, as if coffee here were unusual and exotic also.

"I've had my coffee," he said. "Just the jello, thank you."

"Does Spyro always serve you coffee?" she said, her bitterness returning now against her will as they stood in the kitchen.

"I don't know," he said belligerently.

"But I thought you saw him every evening," she feigned sweet casualness.

"I never notice what he serves," Spence said loudly and indifferently.

"Would you like a large dish or a small dish of jello?" she said heavily.

"Small, for Christ's sake," he told her.

"Gibbs!" she cried. Then, catching herself, she said, "Small it will be, dear."

"What have you got to say that you can't bring it out!" he suddenly turned on her, and taking the dish of jello from her hand he put it down with a bang on the oilcloth covering of the tiny kitchen table.

"Gibbs, let's not have any trouble. Mother has a terrible headache tonight.

"Well, why don't you go to bed then," he said in his stentorian voice.

"Perhaps I will," she said weakly. She sat down and began eating right out of the jello bowl. She ate nearly all the rubbery stiff red imitation strawberry jello and drank in hurried gulps the coffee loaded with condensed milk.

"Spence gave me hell all evening," she said eating. "He thinks I would be happier if I found a fellow!"

She laughed but her laughter brought no response from Gibbs.

"I know I have nothing to offer anybody. Let's face it."

"Why do you have to say *let's face it?*" Gibbs snapped at her.

"Is there something wrong grammatically with it?" she wondered taking her spoon out of her mouth.

"Every dumb son of a bitch in the world is always saying *let's face it.*"

"And your own language is quite refined," she countered.

"Yes, let's face it, it is," he said, a bit weakly, and he took out the harmonica from his pocket, looked at it, and put it down noiselessly on the oilcloth.

"I've always wanted to do right by you, Gibbs. Since you was a little boy, I have tried. But no father around, and all. . . ."

"Mom, we've been over this ten thousand times. Can't

we just forget I didn't have an old man, and you worked like a team of dogs to make up for everything."

"Yes, let's do. Let's forget it all. For heaven's sake, I'm eating all this jello," she said gaily.

"Yes, I noticed," he said.

"But I want to do for you," she told him suddenly again with passion, forgetting everything but her one feeling now, and she put out her hand to him. "You're all I have, Gibbs."

He stared at her. She was weeping.

"I've never been able to do anything for you," she said. "I know I'm not someone you want to bring your friends home to see."

"Mom, for Christ's sake," he said.

"Don't swear," she said. "I may not know grammar or English, but I'm not profane and I never taught you to be. So there," she said, and she brought out her handkerchief and wiped her eyes, making them, he saw, even older and more worn with the rubbing.

"Mom," he said, picking up the harmonica again, "I don't *have* any friends."

"No?" she said laughing a little. Then understanding his remark more clearly as her weeping calmed itself, she said, commanding again, "What do you mean now by that?"

"Just what I said, Mom. I don't have any friends. Except maybe Spyro."

"Oh that Greek boy. We would come back to him."

"How could I have friends, do you think. After all. . . ."

"Don't you go to college like everybody else," she said hurriedly. "Aren't we making the attempt, Gibbs?"

"Don't get so excited. I don't care because I don't have any friends. I wasn't accusing you of anything."

"You go to college and you ought to have friends," she said. "Isn't that right?"

"Look, for Christ's sake, just going to college doesn't bring you friends. Especially a guy like me with...."

"What's wrong with you," she said. "You're handsome. You're a beautiful boy."

"Mom, Je-sus."

"No wonder that Greek is painting you. You're a fine-looking boy."

"Oh it isn't that way at all," he said, bored. "Spyro has to paint somebody."

"I don't know why you don't have friends," she said. "You have everything. Good looks, intelligence, and you can speak and act refined when you want to...."

"You have to be rich at that college. And your parents have to be...."

"Is that *all* then?" she said, suddenly very white and facing him.

"Mom, I didn't mean anything about you. I didn't say any of this to make you feel...."

"Be quiet," she said. "Don't talk."

"Maybe we *should* talk about it, Mom."

"I can't help what happened. What was *was*, the past is the past. Whatever wrong I may have done, the circumstances of your birth, Gibbs...."

"Mom, please, this isn't about you at all."

"I've stood by you, Gibbs," she hurried on as if testifying before a deaf judge. "You can never deny that." She stared at him as though she had lost her reason.

"I'd like to have seen those rich women with their fat manicured husbands do what I've done," she said now as though powerless to stop, words coming out of her mouth that she usually kept and nursed for her long nights of sleeplessness and hate.

She stood up quickly as if to leave the room.

"With no husband or father to boot in this house! I'd like to see *them* do what I did. God damn them," she said.

Gibbs waited there, pale now as she was, and somehow much smaller before her wrath.

"God damn everybody!" she cried. "God damn everybody."

She sat down and began weeping furiously.

"I can't help it if you don't have friends," she told him, quieting herself with a last supreme effort. "I can't help it at all."

"Mom," he said. He wanted to weep too, but there was something too rocklike, too bitter and immovable inside him to let the tears come loose. Often at night as he lay in his bed knowing that Merta was lying in the next room sleepless, he had wanted to get up and go to her and let them both weep together, but he could not.

"Is there anything I could do to change things here at home for you?" she said suddenly wiping away the tears, and tensing her breast to keep more of the torrent from gathering inside herself. "Anything at all I can do, I will," she said.

"Mom," he said, and he got up and as he did so the harmonica fell to the linoleum floor.

"You dropped your little . . . toy," she said tightening her mouth.

"It's not a toy," he began. "This is," he began again. "You see, this is the kind the professionals play on the stage . . . and everywhere."

"I see," she said, struggling to keep the storm within her

quiet, the storm that now if it broke might sweep everything within her away, might rage and rage until only
dying itself could stop it.

"Play something on it, Gibbs darling," she said.

He wanted to ask her if she was all right.

"Play, play," she said desperately.

"What do you want me to play, Mom?" he said, deathly
pale.

"Just play any number you like," she suggested.

He began then to play "How High the Moon" but his
lips trembled too much.

"Keep playing," she said beating her hands with the
heavy veins and the fingers without rings or embellish-
ment.

He looked at her hands as his lips struggled to keep
themselves on the tiny worn openings of the harmonica
which he had described as the instrument of the professionals.

"What a funny tune," she said. "I never listened to it
right before. What did you say they called it?"

"Mom," he said. "Please!"

He stretched out his hand.

"Don't now, don't," she commanded. "Just play. Keep
playing."

Night and Day

"The chestnut man will be here before too long," Cleo said, "and I will buy you a lot of nice chestnuts before bedtime. But you must be a good boy, you must not tell Grandy things Mama says when we're alone together. After lunch tomorrow maybe he will take you out for a walk around the park. Won't that be nice?"

But he just sat there, on the new Persian rug, with his little train and engine, also new like the rug, and also gifts from Grandy, and would not answer her.

There was always the difficulty of his going to sleep, and the best thing was to just let him lie in bed talking to the animals on the wall, talking sometimes half the night.

One night, when Grandy made her tell him she was going to have the animals painted off the walls if he didn't behave, he had put up a fuss and said he was going to tell Grandy what she had called the old man the night he had not given her enough money. After that he got to talk to the kangaroo for an hour and told him what Mama had called Grandy, and then he told his other favorite, the elephant that stood on the weighing machine, and finally he told the South American foxes.

57

Tonight the chestnut man had not come, and when there was unexpectedly no sound from the little room upstairs, Cleo, once the tension had let up, began crying a little and said to Grandy: "His father will never know what bringing up a child means. And wouldn't care maybe if he knew."

Grandy patted her hand lightly.

"Where do you suppose Bruce is anyhow," she said, coldly angry. "It's going on two years."

"Cleo," Grandy said, "you know as well as I the only thing you can do."

They sat down then to their supper of cold chicken, cheese casserole, and cup after cup of coffee ready to strengthen her.

She had just put some food into her mouth when the door upstairs opened and he screamed.

Going up immediately to his room and sitting down with the perfunctory motions of a sleepwalker, she said: "Why can't you control yourself for just one meal."

"Where is Grandy?" he wondered.

"Grandy is reading the paper," she told him.

"I want to see Grandy."

"Well, he is too old and tired to come up the steps all the time."

"Tell Grandy to come up."

"You go to sleep."

She went down again and sat with Grandy and he began to smooth her hair as was his custom.

"Please, please," Cleo said when he kissed her loudly. "Let's try to be a little more careful now."

"Has he been careful?"

"Bruce?" she said, knowing, of course, that it was Bruce he meant.

Grandy watched her as though commanding her to give the answer he wanted.

"I loved Bruce, Grandy. I really did."

"He deserted *you*," Grandy said.

"Oh, now, father, father." She was weak with him.

"I know my own son," he told her. "Bruce ran out on you."

"There is no proof of that, father." Then: "Oh, *Bruce, Bruce*," she said, pretending she was saying this to herself.

"Bruce is no-account, never was, and it's infantile to ever expect his return."

"You shouldn't even think such a thing about your own boy," Cleo said unemphatically.

"Have Grandy come up now!" the small voice from upstairs called.

"He listens to everything we say and do," Cleo told the old man.

"And understands nothing, just like Bruce."

"But you *love* him, don't you," she said, fear in her voice, and her face suddenly red under the lamplight.

"Who?" Grandy roared.

"Who but the boy!" she said rather hotly.

"You know who I love," he told Cleo, and he put his hand on her lap. "And I know who you love."

"Oh, Grandy, Grandy." She was pliant and soft again.

"Why must it always be *Grandy*," the old man said. "Why can't it be. . . ."

"Have Grandy come up, Mama; have him do that now. I am so lonesome."

"Talk to the little kangaroo until you go to sleep, lover," she called up. "Tell the little kangaroo your thoughts."

"No, I'm tired of *him*," the child said. "I want a new animal for telling my thoughts to," he called angrily.

"He wants a police dog," Cleo told the old man.

"They want everything," he replied, holding her hand tightly.

"Like some other people in this world," Cleo said, not removing her hand.

"You can't go on like this," Grandy emphasized to her, peremptorily removing his hand from hers and placing it on her cheek, where it stroked back and forth insinuatingly near her ear like a mouth whispering messages.

"What would our lives be like, if I did this terrible thing," Cleo said.

"You've already gone more than half the way," Grandy said.

"Oh, Grandy," she cried, and she pushed her face into his vest and cried a little.

"If Bruce ever knew, my God, my God." Her voice came muffled and weak from against his chest.

"And what do you think Bruce might be doing tonight?" He was cool and unmoved.

"Well, he's not with my *mother*," she gasped, weakly impetuous, as though this were her last outburst of concern, for immediately after she sank back into his arms, and he kissed her with real feeling.

"Where are you now?" The voice came from upstairs.

"Oh, is he out of his bed, do you think?" Cleo asked, jumping up.

"Sit down, Cleo," the old man commanded. "Nothing is going to surprise us. You're jumpy as a cat. Do sit down, and don't get up again."

"I wish that boy had a nurse sometimes."

"He could have," Grandy told her.

"Oh, dear, dear. What *is* it all about?"

"Don't talk like one of those religious philosophers now," Grandy said to her. "You know and I know what is going to happen." He kissed her on the mouth.

"I don't know, and you can't make me," she said weakly. He kissed her again.

"What is it, then, my *age*," he asked ironically.

"Your age?" She laughed. "Have I ever known a younger man?" She touched his mouth, and he clasped her hand tightly at this.

"Younger than Bruce," he said, and his coy, crafty wink made her tense.

"Grandy, we might destroy everything!" she cautioned.

"You forget Bruce has already done that. How long has he been gone?" He began counting with that theatrical manner he so often assumed now.

"I can't helping thinking Bruce loved me," she said ignoring his manner.

"And his supposed love is enough."

"But for God's sake," she said getting up and pacing about the room. "You're his *father!* Grandy, you're Bruce's father!"

"How many times have you seen Bruce in the last two years—do you remember?" he asked now, his theatrical manner stronger than ever.

"He's been gone, of course, a little more than a year this time."

"*This* time!" Grandy stood up now and walked over to her. He embraced her with passion. Everything else he did resembled different people doing different things successively. But his embraces were his own. Perhaps that is what made her go on with them.

"More than a year, Cleo!" he said, almost shaking her.

"Do you realize how ridiculous that is. Your own husband. Why a year? Why a month? Why even a fortnight? Why should that be?" He actually shook her now. "Why?"

"Please, please, don't wake the child again now. He's been quiet for nearly half an hour."

"Bruce can take *him!*" he said with great suddenness.

"Grandy!" she cried. "Why, you must know me better than that. Why, Grandy!"

She moved out of his orbit, her mouth trembling with surprise, her face a hot, red moon of hurt and confusion.

"Of course, I didn't mean that just as it sounded."

"You did too." She turned on him. "How dare you! Grandy, how dare you!"

She wept a little and, finding no handkerchief, she accepted the one he handed her.

"Give up that little thing upstairs," she began. "I hate you for that talk." Then softening a little again: "Oh, Grandy, Grandy, what *am* I going to do?"

"Do you want to answer this question," he cleared his throat, the actor playing now the counselor-at-law, closing the case. "Where would you have been this past year without my help? How would the little prince upstairs have eaten and slept, do you think? Who would have had the artist to paint the animals on his bedroom wall?"

"Stop all of this talk at once," she said without conviction. "Oh, Grandy." She collapsed.

He held her hand as though this gesture were the source of his power and her weakness.

"You're not a working-woman type, Cleo," he told her, his mouth to her ear now. He kissed her softly and insistently.

"I'm not very clever, if that's what you mean," she said, wiping her tears on his handkerchief again.

"You're not clever in the world's view. You're not a modern woman, Cleo. You belong at home with a man who can take care of you. You aren't meant to make your own way. . . . But that's right what you're going to be doing, if you go on with Bruce! My patience. . . ." He thundered now.

"Oh, no, Grandy," she sobbed. "Don't speak like this. We have to think. . . ."

"You've said that for months. What do we have to think about?"

"Maybe there are circumstances we don't understand," she begged him. "Maybe there's something happened to Bruce we don't know about."

"You forget you're talking about my son."

"That doesn't mean anything here," she said, some of her old thoughts awakening suddenly, only to fade to extinguishment under his touch.

"I know Bruce better than anybody in the world," he emphasized.

"You know him as a man," she said.

"I'm his father," Grandy said.

"You're a man." She was implacable.

"All right, you love Bruce then," he told her.

"I didn't say that. I didn't say that at all." A wave of weakness, impotence, idiocy swept over her again.

"Then what do you mean?" He was insistent.

"All I meant," she said, her breath coming heavily and fear changing her voice so that it resembled both a child's and an old woman's, "all I meant is, are we being fair to *them*, are we. . . ."

"Tell me this," he said, holding her hand with savage firmness. "Does Bruce love you?"

She drew back, as though this question, never posed

before, had swept away everything of the little she had held back for herself.

"Grandy, please, do we have to be so . . . so specific?"

"Yes, Cleo, yes."

"What was your question then?" she said, reaching for her cigarettes.

"Here," he commanded, "take one of mine."

"I'd rather have one of my. . . ."

He put the cigarette in her mouth and lit it.

"Now, Cleo, I also can be of another mind. . . ."

"About what?" she said, looking at him with her terrified, young-innocent-girl face.

"There is a limit to *my* time, *my* endurance. And I'm not going to live forever, after all. I want life now. Not tomorrow. And I've waited. . . ."

"Grandy, just don't do anything rash yet. Please wait, things will straighten out, I know. . . ."

"Have you ever thought that I might have somebody else, too?" he said.

"Yes," she said, trying to steady the fear that made her voice muffled as though she were speaking to him through a curtain. "I've thought of that, Grandy . . . many times." She lifted her tear-stained face to him.

"Think of it tonight with special clearness," he ordered her.

"I will, Grandy," she said, the tears falling again now, and she noticed that he did not caress her, did not hold out a hand to her. He had given her the question, the final decision; he was not going to do more. She saw that she must answer.

"It's the most difficult thing in the world, Grandy."

"Bawling's not going to help you, not going to get you anywhere." He was like another man now, and she saw something in him at that moment, vague and far away, which must have destroyed happiness for her with his son Bruce.

"I must know *now*," he told her.

"Oh, Grandy, no." She wept now, unashamed, uncontrolled.

"Of course," she said incoherently, "it's you, Grandy."

"And if it's me, then, it can't be him."

"You mean Bruce," she said, looking up from her hands which she had put over her face, hopefully expectant.

"I mean the kid!" He was clear and complete.

"What are you saying," she said, suddenly calm, her tears suddenly gone, a white toneless face, stripped of every emotion, looking at him.

"I want to marry *you*. Let Bruce have the kid."

"He's not a kid," she said.

"Well, what the hell is he?"

"He's still almost an infant." She walked up and down the room.

"And you will go to work to support him then?"

She did not say anything.

"I asked you a question, Cleo. Will you go to work in a factory or office to support him?"

"I never knew before how cruel you really are, and *were*."

"I've waited for you for at least two years, and I can't wait any longer." His voice quieted down slowly.

"I think I am beginning to see how it would be," she said and walked to the other side of the room and sat down.

"What was the meaning of that cryptic remark?"

"There was nothing cryptic in it, and it was more than a remark. I think it was a decision."

"You've made a decision?" He smiled knowingly.

"I think I have," she said.

He laughed.

"I must try to be calm, though," she told him. "I must say only what I mean and no more."

"That would be unusual for you." He used all his bitterness.

"Would it, Grandy?" She looked at him and as he gazed at her he hardly recognized her. She hardly, perhaps, recognized herself.

"What then have I been doing these years?" she said. "My God, yes, what."

"Now, Cleo, what is this?" he said going over to the chair where she was sitting.

"Don't come near me," she ordered him, and there was a strength in the way she motioned to him with trembling, thin hands covered with his rings.

"I see everything, of course, I've always seen it," she told him. "I think I see myself."

"You sound just like Bruce now," he said. "The goddam old preacher in him has come out in you."

"Just words," she said. "Just your old words." She stood up. "Words from an old goat," she cried, looking at his white hair.

"Cleo," he admonished, with gay good humor. "Realize what you are saying, my dear."

"What does that mean, realize what I'm saying. I'm *realizing* you, for the love of God. Don't you know that?"

"And what does that mean?" he said, and his disguise, or disguises, suddenly to her seemed to fall like pieces of cardboard at their feet. She felt she almost heard a sound of collapse in the room.

"An old old goat on his last legs, making a bargain as hard ... as hard. ..." she said.

"Cleo, you know if you finish saying this, there can be nothing more for the two of us. Consider well what you are going to say."

He held up his hand.

"Oh the theater of *that!*" She almost spat, her handsome face suddenly ugly.

At that moment they heard the bare feet and saw the child come into the room, or rather they did not see him. They both looked and looked away as though, after all, he had been there from the beginning.

The boy clasped his mother around the waist, but she went on talking, her hand, which had always fallen automatically on his curls when he went up close to her, suddenly now raised at the old man.

"You hit Grandy! Mama you hit Grandy!" the child cried, and he ran between her and his grandfather.

"Stop, don't touch him," she told the child. She went over to where the boy stood and brought him back to her.

"He's not your Grandy any more," she roared at him.

"Cleo, I can and I will make trouble for you if you speak in front of that boy."

"You old goat," she cried, and her hand now fell on the head of her son.

"You whoring old goat!"

Mrs. Benson

"I don't know why Mrs. Carlin entertained," Mrs. Benson admitted. "She didn't like it, and she couldn't do it."

"I had to sit an entire hour under one of those potted palms she had in her house," Mrs. Benson's daughter, Wanda, recalled. "There was a certain odor about it— whether from the soil, or the plant, or the paper about the container. I felt terribly uncomfortable."

The two women, Wanda Walters, unmarried and thirty, from Philadelphia, and her mother, who lived in Europe, and had been married many times, and who was now Mrs. Benson, had nearly finished their tea, in an English tearoom within walking distance from the American Express, in Paris.

Mrs. Benson had known the English tearoom for many years, though she could never exactly remember its French name, and so could not ever recommend it to her friends, and she and her daughter, when they had their yearly reunions in Paris, always came to it. Their meeting in Paris this year had been rather a prolonged one, owing to Wanda's having failed to get a return passage to the

States, and it had been a summer that was hot, humid, and gray—and not eventful for either of them.

This year, too, they found themselves going less and less anywhere at all, and they were somewhat embarrassed— at least, Mrs. Benson said *she* was—to find that they spent the better part of the day in the English tearoom, talking, for the most part, about people they had both known in Philadelphia twenty-odd years ago, when Wanda had been "little," and when Mrs. Benson—well, as she said, had at least had a different name!

It was the first time in many years, perhaps *the* first, that Mrs. Benson had really talked with her daughter at length about anything (they had always *traveled* before, as the older woman said), and certainly the first time in Wanda's memory that they had talked at all about "back home," as Mrs. Benson now called it with a chilly, condescending affection. And if their French or American friends happened by now, Mrs. Benson, if not Wanda, expressed by a glance or word a certain disappointment that their "talk" must be interrupted.

Mrs. Benson had made it a fixed practice not to confide in her daughter (she had once said to a close friend of hers: "I don't know my daughter, and it's a bit too late to begin!"), but the name *Mrs. Carlin,* which had come into their conversation so haphazardly, as if dropped from the awning of the café, together with the gloominess of their Paris, had set Mrs. Benson off. *Mrs. Carlin* came to open up a mine of confidences and single isolated incidents.

This was interesting to Wanda because Mrs. Benson had always been loath to "tell," to reminisce. Mrs. Benson hated anecdotes, regarding them as evidence of senility in the old, and cretinism in the young, and though there were other people "back home," of course, Mrs.

Carlin could easily carry them through for the rest of Paris, and the potted palms, which had so dismayed Wanda, seemingly set Mrs. Benson "right" at last.

"I don't suppose you remember when they were popular," Mrs. Benson referred to the palms. "But they were once nearly everywhere. I've always disliked them, and, I think, perhaps, I even vaguely *fear* them."

"I don't think Mrs. Carlin *liked* them," Wanda said abruptly, so abruptly that Mrs. Benson dropped a long ash from her cigarette into her tea, and then called the waiter.

"How on earth do you know Mrs. Carlin didn't like them?" Mrs. Benson flushed slightly and then paused while the waiter brought her a fresh cup.

Wanda paused also. She felt that her mother did not *want* to know that she knew anything about Mrs. Carlin, and Wanda, in any case, was not very much interested in explaining what she did mean.

"I simply meant this," Wanda felt she must explain, under the *look* her mother gave her. "The part of the house Mrs. Carlin used for *entertainment* could not have reflected *anybody's* taste."

Mrs. Benson opened her eyes wide, and brought her mouth into a kind of cupid's bow. Then, in a voice quieter than her expression, she said: "I'd have to say, Wanda, that you were right!"

"But how on earth did you *know?*" Mrs. Benson suddenly brought out, and she looked at her daughter as if a fresh light had been thrown on the latter's character also.

"What I think I meant," Wanda began again, tearing apart one of the tiny envelopes of sugar that lay beside her spoon, "Mrs. Carlin was, as we both know, more than a *little* wealthy . . ."

Mrs. Benson cleared her throat, but then decided, evidently, not to speak, and her silence was as emphatic as she could make it.

"That is," Wanda went on slowly, "she could *afford* to entertain rather shabbily."

"Rather *shabbily?*" Mrs. Benson considered this. "That is a terribly queer word for *her*."

"But you yourself . . ."

"I don't like potted palms," Mrs. Benson pushed through to what was, as her face showed, the important matter here, "and I don't like all those original early 19th-century landscapes with cattle," she became now as firm as if in court, "but as to her house being *shabby*. . . ."

"*Depressing* then," Wanda said. "It was certainly depressing."

Mrs. Benson laughed, guardedly indulgent. "You're so hard on the poor dear," she said in a tone of voice unlike her own.

"But I thought you thought as I did," Wanda cried. "About *her*, at least!" Displeasure and boredom rang in her voice, but there was an even stronger expression there of confusion and doubt.

"I do, and I don't," Mrs. Benson put endearment and confidence now into her voice. Then, unaccountably, she looked at her rings. She had many. They were, without doubt, too genuine, if anything, and as they shone in the later afternoon light, they made her mother look, Wanda felt, both very rich and very old.

"I think you're right, though," Wanda heard Mrs. Benson's voice continuing, "right about Mrs. Carlin's not caring whether she impressed *people* or not."

"I don't know if I quite meant that," Wanda told her mother, but under her breath now. "I mean only she didn't care whether they *enjoyed* themselves or not at her house."

They were both silent for a moment, as if surprised at the difficulties which had suddenly sprung up from nowhere, difficulties that were so obscure in themselves, and yet which offered some kind of threat of importance.

"The potted palms were a fright, of course," Mrs. Benson seemed either conciliatory or marking time. "And even for potted palms, they were dreadful." She touched her daughter's arm lightly. "They looked *dead*."

Going on, Mrs. Benson added: "I always thought of old-fashioned small-town Greek candy-kitchens when I saw those palm trees at Mrs. Carlin's. And her strange little painted-glass player piano, too!"

"I never saw *that*," Wanda admitted. She looked away from her mother's expression.

"Oh, you've forgotten it, is all," Mrs. Benson said. "It played for *all* the guests, that player piano . . . at least once." She laughed. "Mrs. Carlin seldom invited anybody twice."

Mrs. Benson had a peculiar, oblique, faraway look in her eyes, a look Wanda did not remember quite ever having seen on her mother's face before—indeed, on anybody's face.

Then, suddenly clearing her throat, Mrs. Benson coughed ceremoniously, struggling perhaps with a decision.

The one thing, Wanda remembered again, the thing that her mother disliked so much in others, was stories, *anecdotes*—indeed any narration which was prolonged beyond the length of a paragraph. But usually when Mrs. Benson cleared her throat *and* coughed, she was going to tell something which was important and necessary, if not long, or anecdotal.

But then, quickly, as if she had been given a reprieve of some kind, Mrs. Benson cried: "Oh, it's all so *nothing!*" and poured herself some tea.

"But what else was there?" Wanda cried, annoyance and curiosity both in her voice. Mrs. Benson shook her head.

"You did have something special, I believe," Wanda was positive.

"Oh, not actually," Mrs. Benson said. Then, with her faraway look again, she managed to say, "I *was* remembering an afternoon—oh, a long, long time ago at Mrs. Carlin's. . . . But in a *different* part of the house, you see."

Wanda waited, suddenly touched with something stronger than curiosity. But she knew that if she so much as moved now, Mrs. Benson might remember her own horror of anecdotes, and would close up tight.

"I dread to think how long ago that actually was," Mrs. Benson continued carefully, and her eyes then strayed out to the street, where a bus was slowing down to stop for a woman and a small child.

Mrs. Benson waited for the woman and child to board the bus, then commencing again: "I can't believe that it was so long ago as 1935, I mean, or along in there. . . . But, Mrs. Carlin had already begun to entertain her guests in one part of the house . . . and to *live* herself in another! She had begun dividing up her life in that way!"

She smiled at Wanda, almost in the manner of one who had finished her story there.

Wanda nodded only enough to let her mother know she was listening.

"I don't care much for this *tea*, today," Mrs. Benson said suddenly in an unexpectedly loud voice, and she looked up and about the room.

When Wanda said nothing, but showed that she was

waiting, Mrs. Benson drank some more of the tea she did not like, and said: "Mrs. Carlin had never, I think, been particularly interested in *me*, as distinct from the others, until your father left me. . . . Evidently, *she* had never been too happy in her marriage, either . . . I gathered that from something she once let drop. . . ."

"However," Mrs. Benson said, raising the empty tea cup, and looking up under at the bottom of it hurriedly, "however, she wanted me to see things. I knew that. She wanted me to see the things—the part of the house, you understand, that the *others* never saw."

Wanda nodded, a kind of fleeting awareness in her face.

"That was when she called me, well *aside*, I suppose one would have to say, and said something to me like, '*I want to really have you in some time, Rose.*'"

It came as a sort of shock to Wanda to hear her mother's Christian name. She had not only not heard it for many years—she had actually forgotten it, so separate had their two lives, and their very names, become.

But Mrs. Benson had gone right on now through her daughter's surprise, or shock: "At first I hadn't quite understood what Mrs. Carlin meant, you see. . . . She had taken hold of my arm, gently, and let me out of the room where she had always entertained the *others*. We got into a small gold elevator, and were gone in a minute. . . . When we got out, well—let me assure you, there wasn't a potted palm in the place!

"It was another house, another atmosphere, another place and time!"

A look of something like pain crossed Wanda's face, but her mother missed this in her final decision to "tell."

"It was a bit incredible to me then, and it's more so now," Mrs. Benson anticipated her daughter's possible incredulity, or indifference.

Pausing briefly, it was Mrs. Benson's turn now to study her daughter's face critically, but evidently, at the last, she found nothing on the younger woman's face to stop her.

Still, Mrs. Benson waited, looking at nothing in particular, while the waiter removed the empty cups, wiped the marble swiftly with a small cloth, bowed vaguely, and muttering part of a phrase, left.

Mrs. Benson commented perfunctorily on the indulgence of French waiters and French cafés, pointing out how wonderful it was to be able to stay *forever* when one wanted to.

Outside the light was beginning to fail, and a slight breeze came across to them from the darkening boulevard.

Wanda moved suddenly and unceremoniously in her chair, and Mrs. Benson fixed her with a new and indeterminate expression.

Raising her voice, almost as if to reach the street, Mrs. Benson said: "A week after Mrs. Carlin had showed me the 'real' part of the house, she invited me again, in an invitation she had written in her own hand, and which I must have somewhere, still. . . . I had never had a *written* invitation before from her, nobody had . . . always telephoned ones. . . . It was a dark January afternoon, I recall, and I was feeling, well, at that time, pretty low. . . . In the *new* part of the house—and I couldn't get over this time its *immensity*—tea was never mentioned, thank God, and we had some wonderful ancient Portuguese brandy. . . . But as we sat there talking, I kept hearing something soft but arresting. . . ."

Mrs. Benson stopped now in the guise of one who hears only what she is describing.

"Looking back away from Mrs. Carlin," Mrs. Benson said, "in the furthest part of the room, I was quite taken aback to see some actual *musicians*. Mrs. Carlin had an entire small string orchestra playing there for her. . . . You know, I thought I was mistaken. I thought it was perhaps a large oil, a mural, or something. . . . But Mrs. Carlin touched my hand just then, and said, '*They're for you, Rose.*'"

Mrs. Benson pressed her daughter's hand lightly at that, as if to convey by some touch *part* of the reality of that afternoon.

"I think she wanted to *help* me," Mrs. Benson said in a flat plain voice now, and with a helpless admission of anticlimax. "Your father—as I said, had just *gone,* and I think she knew how everything stood."

Mrs. Benson avoided her daughter's glance by looking at her hands, which she held before her again now, so that there was the sudden quick scintillation again, and then went on: "When Mrs. Carlin took me to the door that day, I knew she wanted to say something else, something still more *helpful,* if you will, and I was afraid she was going to say what in fact she did."

Wanda's open-eyed expression made her mother suddenly smile.

"It was nothing sensational, my dear, or alarming! Mrs. Carlin was never *that!*"

"Well, for heaven's sake, then," Wanda cried.

"I said it was nothing sensational." In Mrs. Benson's dread of the *anecdote*—the inevitable concomitant of old age—she had so often told people nothing at all, and safety still, of course, lay in being silent. But as Wanda watched Mrs. Benson struggle there, postponing the telling of what she would have liked so much to tell, she realized in part what the struggle meant: Mrs. Benson had invariably all her life told her daughter *nothing*.

But Mrs. Benson had gone on again: "Mrs. Carlin was

still beautiful then, and as I see now, *young*. . . . And I rather imagine that when she was very young, and when there had been, after all, a Mr. Carlin. . . ."

A look from Wanda sped Mrs. Benson on: "I don't know *why* I treasure what Mrs. Carlin said to me," she hurried faster now. "But it is one of the few things that any other human being ever said to me that I do hold on to."

Mrs. Benson looked at the *addition* which the waiter had left, and her lips moved slightly over what was written there.

"Mrs. Carlin said to me," she went on, still looking at the waiter's bill, although her eyes were closed, " 'You're the only one who could *possibly* be asked in here with me, my dear. . . . I couldn't have the *others,* and I knew I couldn't have them. . . . They're not for *us* . . . And if you should ever feel you would like to *stay on,*' Mrs. Carlin said, *'why don't you, my dear?'* "

"She actually thought so well of you!" Wanda said, and then hearing the metallic hardness of her own voice, lowered her eyes in confusion.

"Of course, that was a long time ago," Mrs. Benson said vaguely, more of a cold edge now in her voice. "She wouldn't want *anyone* there now," she added.

"She is such a recluse then?" Wanda asked. Mrs. Benson did not answer. She had taken some francs out of her purse and was staring at them.

"Some of this money," she pointed out, "have you noticed? It comes to pieces in one's hands. I hardly know what to do with some of the smaller notes."

"These little reunions in Paris are such a pleasure, Mother," Wanda said in a rather loud, bright voice.

"Are they, my dear?" Mrs. Benson answered in her old

firm manner. Then, in a sudden hard voice: "I'm so glad if they are."

The two women rose from the table at the same time, Mrs. Benson having deposited some of the notes on the marble-topped table, and they moved toward the front of the café, and into the street.

Sermon

Ladies and people, you must realize, or you would not be sitting here before me, that I am the possessor of your ears. Don't speak, I will talk. You have sat here before, and have heard things men, or in some cases, ladies told you. I have no intention of telling you the same things, but will proceed just as though you were all in the privacy of your own bathhouses. I was not called here to entertain you. You could entertain yourselves if you weren't here. The fact you are here means something. (I will not mention the fact of my being here.) We face one another across the hostile air, you waiting to hear and to criticize, and I half-staring at some of you and not seeing the rest of you, though perhaps wanting to. Some of you are rude. Many of you are old and homely, others are not up to the speech I have in readiness. We *all* of us know *all* of this. It is in the *air* I look through to see you. Yet we all feel we have to go on. You have left the comfort of your living rooms and bathhouses to be here. I have come because I am a speaker and had to. None of us are really happy, none of us are in the place he feels he might want to be. Many of you feel there must be a better place for

79

you than the one you are occupying now. There is a feeling of everything being not quite right. You feel if you only knew more or could do more you would be somewhere else. The fact is, however, you are wrong.

I say this looking at all of you now. You are wrong, and I am powerless to add or subtract from that fact. You came originally wrong, and you have been getting worse in every way since that day. There is, in fact, no hope for you, and there never was. Even if you had never been born there would have been no hope for you. It was hopeless whether you arrived or not. Yet you all arrived, you got here, you are *here*. And it is all so meaningless, because you all know there is a better place for you than here. And that is the trouble.

You will not accept the *hereness*. You will not accept me. Yet I am the only thing there is under the circumstances, but you reject me, and why—well I will tell you why. Because you have nothing better to do or be than the person you are now, occupying the particular chair you now occupy and which you are not improving by occupying. You have improved nothing since you came into this situation. You have tried to improve yourself, of course, or things connected with yourself, but you have only finished in making everything worse, you have only finished in making yourself worse than when you were sent, worse than what you were when you were born, worse even than what you were before you entered this great Amphitheater.

There is, in short, no hope for you, as I said earlier. You are bad off and getting more so, and sadly enough when you get in the worst shape of all so that you think you will not be able to go on for another second, the road ahead is still worse yet. For there is no hope for you even when things get so impossibly terrible that you will kill yourself. For that is no solution. In death you will only begin where you left off, but naturally, in worse shape.

Yet you continue to sit here watching me, like skinned tadpoles whose long-dead brains still send messages to your twitching feet. You twitch as you listen to me but you hear nothing. You have never heard anything.

And now you are waiting for the message, the solution to all my speech. You have been thinking, "What He says is terrible and frightening, but now will come the Good Part, the part with the meaning . . ." Ladies and people, listen to me. I have no Good Part to give you. My only message, if it can be called one, and I do not call it one, I call it nothing, my message to you is there is no message. You have made a terrible mistake in coming to the Amphitheater tonight to hear Me, yet you would have made a mistake no matter what you did tonight for the simple reason that you have no choice but to make mistakes, because you have no plans. You are going somewhere because you think you have to . . . That is what you are doing, and how therefore could you do anything but make mistakes. You continue to act and you have nothing to act with but the actions. Hence you are doomed to lectures and books hoping to save yourselves in the evening. Another attempt at action. You are doomed because you will go on trying to be other than you are and therefore you succeed always in continuing as you have been. There is no choice. You are listening even now with your pathetic tadpole faces because you know you are not getting my words. Give up trying, dear auditors. Be without trying to be. Lay back in your seats and let the air have its way with you. Let it tickle you in the spots where you are always fighting its insistent moisture. Don't let it retreat.

Let things be. Don't try to be improved by my speech, because nothing can improve you. Surrender to what you are continuing *against,* and perhaps you will not have to go ahead with everything. And I know how weary you are of going ahead. Oh, don't I know it.

You are beginning to look at the Giant Clocks, meaning you have stood all you can for one night. I do not pity or sympathize with you and at the same time I do, because you do not belong here, as I said earlier. Nobody belongs here. It has all been a mistake your coming here. I, of course, am a Mistake, and how could my coming be a success. Yet in a sense it *is,* ladies and people, for the simple reason that I have prepared no speech and have not thought about what I am saying to you. I knew it would be hopeless. I knew when I saw your faces that you would only listen to what you say to yourself in your bathhouses or your laundry cleanup kitchens. You knew everything anyhow and have continued to improve on what has already been done. Hence you are hopeless.

I have talked here tonight in the hope you would not hear, because if you didn't you might not so thoroughly disgust yourselves, and therefore me. But you have sat in exactly the rapport or lack of it which I expect from the human tadpole. You have been infinitely repulsive to me, and for that I thank you, because by being infinitely repulsive you have continued continuity and what more could any speaker ask. What if you had become while I was talking. The whole world would have changed, of course. You would have all become alive. But the truth of the continuum is that it is continuous. You have not failed History, the continuous error. You have gone on with it, but *continuing.*

And so I say to you, pale and yet red tadpoles, you are

hopeless and my words are spoken to tell you not to hope. You have nothing with which to win. It is doom itself that I see your bloated eyes and mouths begging for. How could I say anything to you then but to return to you the stale air which you have been breathing in my face all evening. I return it to you, therefore, not in flatulence, that would be to flatter you, but in air in return. And I thank you. I *mean* this. I thank you one and all, ladies and people. I take pleasure in my activity though I know you do not, are not expected to take any and would be miserable if my pleasure became real to you. And so farewell, or rather good-by, because we will meet again. There is no escape from it. That is why we are all so repulsive to one another: infinitely so. Life is immortal. Its eggs are too numerous for it but to spawn at the mere touch, and therefore with real emotion I say *So be it*. Come whenever you can, I am always here. Good-by, and yet not good-by.

GOD

Everything Under the Sun

"I don't like to make things hard for you," Jesse said to Cade, "but when you act like this I don't know what's going to happen. You don't like nothing I do for you anyhow."

The two boys, Jesse and Cade, shared a room over the south end of State Street. Jesse had a job, but Cade, who was fifteen, seldom could find work. They were both down to their last few dollars.

"I told you a man was coming up here to offer me a job," Cade said.

"You can't wait for a man to come offering you a job," Jesse said. He laughed. "What kind of a man would that be anyhow."

Cade laughed too because he knew Jesse did not believe anything he said.

"This man did promise me," Cade explained, and Jesse snorted.

"Don't pick your nose like that," Jesse said to Cade. "What if the man seen you picking."

Cade said the man wouldn't care.

"What does this man do?" Jesse wondered.

84

"He said he had a nice line of goods I could sell for him and make good money," Cade replied.

"Good money selling," Jesse laughed. "My advice to you is go out and look for a job, any job, and not wait for no old man to come to teach you to sell."

"Well nobody else wants to hire me due to my face," Cade said.

"What's wrong with your face?" Jesse wanted to know. "Outside of you picking your nose all the time, you have as good a face as anybody's."

"I can't look people in the eye is what," Cade told him.

Jesse got up and walked around the small room.

"Like I told you," Jesse began the same speech he always gave when Cade was out of work, "I would do anything for you on account of your brother. He saved my life in the goddam army and I ain't never going to forget that."

Cade made his little expression of boredom which was to pinch the bridge of his nose.

"But you got to work sometimes!" Jesse exploded. "I don't get enough for two!"

Cade grimaced, and did not let go the bridge of his nose because he knew this irritated Jesse almost as much as his picking did, but Jesse could not criticize him for just holding his nose, and that made him all the angrier.

"And you stay out of them arcades too!" Jesse said to Cade. "Spending the money looking at them pictures," Jesse began. "For the love of. . . ." Suddenly Jesse stopped short.

"For the love of what?" Cade jumped him. He knew the reason that Jesse did not finish the sentence with a swear word was he went now to the Jesus Saves Mission every night, and since he had got religion he had quit being quite so friendly to Cade as before, cooler and more distant, and he talked, like today, about how good work is for everybody.

"That old man at the trucking office should have never told you you had a low IQ," Jesse returned to this difficulty of Cade's finding work.

But this remark did not touch Cade today.

"Jesse," Cade said, "I don't care about it."

"You don't care!" Jesse flared up.

"That's right," Cade said, and he got up and took out a piece of cigarette from his pants cuff, and lit a match to the stub. "I don't believe in IQ's," Cade said.

"Did you get that butt off the street?" Jesse wanted to know, his protective manner making his voice soft again.

"I ain't answering that question," Cade told him.

"Cade, why don't you be nice to me like you used to be," Jesse said.

"Why don't *I* be nice to *you*!" Cade exclaimed with savagery.

Suddenly frightened, Jesse said, "Now simmer down." He was always afraid when Cade suddenly acted too excited.

"You leave me alone," Cade said. "I ain't interferin' with your life and don't you interfere with mine. The little life I have, that is." He grunted.

"I owe something to you and that's why I can't just let you be any old way you feel like being," Jesse said.

"You don't owe me a thing," Cade told him.

"I know who I owe and who I don't," Jesse replied.

"You always say you owe me on account of my brother saved your life just before he got hisself blowed up."

"Cade, you be careful!" Jesse warned, and his head twitched as he spoke.

"I'm glad he's gone," Cade said, but without the emotion he usually expressed when he spoke of his brother. He had talked against his brother so long in times past in order to get Jesse riled up that it had lost nearly all meaning for both of them. "Yes, sir, I don't care!" Cade repeated.

Jesse moved his lips silently and Cade knew he was praying for help.

Jesse opened his eyes wide then and looking straight at Cade, twisted his lips, trying not to let the swear words come out, and said: "All right, Cade," after a long struggle.

"And if religion is going to make you close with your money," Cade began looking at Jesse's mouth, "close and *mean*, too, then I can clear out of here. I don't need you, Jesse."

"What put the idea into your head religion made me close with my money?" Jesse said, and he turned very pale.

"You need me here, but you don't want to pay what it takes to keep me," Cade said.

Jesse trembling walked over to Cade very close and stared at him.

Cade watched him, ready.

Jesse said, "You can stay here as long as you ever want to. And no questions asked." Having said this, Jesse turned away, a glassy look on his face, and stared at the cracked calcimine of their wall.

"On account of my old brother I can stay!" Cade yelled.

"All right then!" Jesse shouted back, but fear on his face. Then softening with a strange weakness he said, "No, Cade, that's not it either," and he went over and put his arm on Cade's shoulder.

"Don't touch me," Cade said. "I don't want none of that *brother* love. Keep your distance."

"You behave," Jesse said, struggling with his emotion.

"Ever since you give up women and drinking you been picking on me," Cade said. "I do the best I can."

Cade waited for Jesse to say something.

"And you think picking on me all the time makes you get a star in heaven, I suppose," Cade said weakly.

Jesse, who was not listening, walked the length of the cramped little room. Because of the heat of the night and the heat of the discussion, he took off his shirt. On his chest was tattooed a crouched black panther, and on his right arm above his elbow a large unfolding flower.

"I did want to do right by you, but maybe we *had* better part," Jesse said, crossing his arms across his chest. He spoke like a man in his sleep, but immediately he had spoken, a scared look passed over his face.

Cade suddenly went white. He moved over to the window.

"I can't do no more for you!" Jesse cried, alarmed but helpless at his own emotion. "It ain't in me to do no more for you! Can't you see that, Cade. Only so much, no more!"

When there was no answer from Cade, Jesse said, "Do you hear what I say?"

Cade did not speak.

"Fact is," Jesse began again, as though explaining now to himself, "I don't seem to care about nothing. I just want somehow to sit and not move or do nothing. I don't know what it is."

"You never did give a straw if I lived or died, Jesse," Cade said, and he just managed to control his angry tears.

Jesse was silent, as on the evenings when alone in the dark, while Cade was out looking for a job, he had tried to figure out what he should do in his trouble.

"*Fact* is," Cade now whirled from the window, his eyes brimming with tears, "it's all the other way around. I don't need you except for money, but you need me *to tell you who you are!*"

"What?" Jesse said, thunderstruck.

"You know goddam well *what*," Cade said, and he wiped the tears off his face with his fist. "On account of you don't know who you are, that's why."

"You little crumb," Jesse began, and he moved threateningly, but then half remembering his nights at the Mission, he walked around the room, muttering.

"Where are my cigarettes?" Jesse said suddenly. "Did you take them?"

"I thought you swore off when you got religion," Cade said.

"Yeah," Jesse said in the tone of voice more like his old self, and he went up to Cade, who was smoking another butt.

"Give me your smoke," he said to Cade.

Cade passed it to him, staring.

"I don't think you heard what I said about leaving," Cade told Jesse.

"I heard you," Jesse said.

"Well, I'm going to leave you, Jesse. God damn you."

Jesse just nodded from where he now sat on a crate they used as a chair. He groaned a little like the smoke was disagreeable for him.

"Like I say, Jesse," and Cade's face was dry of tears now. "It may be hard for me to earn money, but I know who I am. I may be dumb, but I'm *all together!*"

"Cade," Jesse said sucking on the cigarette furiously. "I didn't mean for you to go. After all, there is a lot between us."

Jesse's fingers moved nervously over the last tiny fragment of the cigarette.

"Do you have any more smokes in your pants cuff or anywhere?" Jesse asked, as though he were the younger and the weaker of the two now.

"I have, but I don't think I should give any to a religious man," Cade replied.

Jesse tightened his mouth.

Cade handed him another of the butts.

"What are you going to offer me, if I do decide to stay," Cade said suddenly. "On account of this time I'm not going to stay if you don't give me an offer!"

Jesse stood up suddenly, dropping his cigarette, the smoke coming out of his mouth as though he had all gone to smoke inside himself.

"What am I going to offer you?" Jesse said like a man in a dream. "What?" he said sleepily.

Then waving his arms, Jesse cried, "All right! Get out!" And suddenly letting go at last he struck Cade across the mouth, bringing some blood. "Now you git," he said. "Git out."

Jesse panted, walking around the room. "You been bleedin' me white for a year. That's the reason I'm the way I am. I'm bled white."

Cade went mechanically to the bureau, took out a shirt, a pair of shorts, a toothbrush, his straight razor, and a small red box. He put these in a small bag such as an athlete might carry to his gym. He walked over to the door and went out.

Below, on the sidewalk, directly under the room where he and Jesse had lived together a year, Cade stood waiting for the streetcar. He knew Jesse was looking down on him. He did not have to wait long.

"Cade," Jesse's voice came from the window. "You get back here, Cade, goddam you." Jesse hearing the first of his profanity let loose at last, swore a lot more then, as though he had found his mind again in swearing.

A streetcar stopped at that moment.

"Don't get on that car, Cade," Jesse cried. "Goddam it."

Cade affected impatience.

"You wait now, goddam you," Jesse said putting on his rose-colored shirt.

"Cade," Jesse began when he was on the street beside his friend. "Let's go somewhere and talk this over. . . . See how I am," he pointed to his trembling arm.

"There ain't nowhere to go since you give up drinking," Cade told him.

Jesse took Cade's bag for him.

"Well if it makes you unhappy, I'll drink with you," Jesse said.

"I don't mind being unhappy," Cade said. "It's *you* that minds, Jesse."

"I want you to forgive me, Cade," Jesse said, putting his hand on Cade's arm.

Cade allowed Jesse's arm to rest there.

"Well, Jesse," Cade said coldly.

"You see," Jesse began, pulling Cade gently along with him as they walked toward a tavern. "You see, I don't know what it is, Cade, but you know everything."

Cade watched him.

They went into the tavern and although they usually sat at the bar, today they chose a table. They ordered beer.

"You see, Cade, I've lied to you, I think, and you're right. Of course your brother did save my life, but you saved it again. I mean you saved it more. You saved me," and he stretched out his trembling arm at Cade.

Jesse seeing the impassive look on Cade's face stopped and then going on as though he did not care whether anybody heard him or not, he said: "You're all I've got, Cade."

Cade was going to say *all right now* but Jesse went on speaking frantically and fluently as he had never spoken before. "You know ever since the war, I've been like I am ... And Cade, I need you that's why ... I know you don't need me," he nodded like an old man now. "But I don't care now. I ain't proud no more about it."

Jesse stopped talking and a globule of spit rested thickly on his mouth.

"I'm cured of being proud, Cade."

"Well, all right then," Cade finally said, folding his arms and compressing his mouth.

"All right?" Jesse said, a silly look on his face, which had turned very young again.

"But you leave me alone now if I stay," Cade said.

"I will," Jesse said, perhaps not quite sure what it was Cade meant. "You can do anything you want, Cade. All I need is to know you won't really run out. No matter what I might some day say or do, you stay, Cade!"

"Then I don't want to hear no more about me getting just any old job," Cade said, drinking a swallow of beer.

"All right," Jesse said. "All right, all right."

"And you quit going to that old Mission and listening to that religious talk."

Jesse nodded.

"I ain't living with no old religious fanatic," Cade said.

Jesse nodded again.

"And there ain't no reason we should give up drinking and all the rest of it at night."

Jesse agreed.

"Or women," Cade said, and he fumbled now with the button of his shirt. It was such a very hot night his hand almost unconsciously pushed back the last button which had held his shirt together, exposing the section of his chest on which rested the tattooed drawing of a crouched black panther, the identical of Jesse's.

"And I don't want to hear no more about me going to work at all for a while," Cade was emphatic.

"All right, then, Cade," Jesse grinned, beginning to giggle and laugh now.

"Well I should say *all right*," Cade replied, and he smiled briefly, as he accepted Jesse's hand which Jesse proferred him then by standing up.

Goodnight, Sweetheart

Pearl Miranda walked stark naked from her classroom in the George Washington School where she taught the eighth grade, down Locust Street, where she waited until some of the cars which had stopped for a red traffic light had driven on, then hurried as fast as her weight could allow her down Smith Avenue.

She waited under a catalpa tree, not yet in leaf, for some men to pass by on the other side of the street. It was fairly dark, but she could not be sure if they would see her.

Hurrying on down Smith Avenue then, she passed a little girl, who called out to her, though the child did not recognize her.

The house she at last turned into was that of Winston Cramer, who gave piano lessons to beginners, and whom she herself had taught in the eighth grade nearly twenty years before.

She rang the doorbell.

She could see Winston beyond the picture window sitting in an easy chair engaged in manicuring his nails.

She rang and rang, but he did not move from his sitting position.

A woman from across the street came out on the porch and stood there watching.

Pearl rapped now on the door, and called Winston's name softly. Then she saw him get up. He looked angry.

"I discontinued the subscription," she heard his cross high voice. "I don't want the *News—*" and he caught sight of her.

He stood looking at her, immobile behind the glass of the door. Then he opened the door cautiously.

"Miss Miranda?"

"Let me in, for pity's sake," she answered him. "It's all right to open the door."

The woman across the street went on standing on her porch looking over at the Cramer house.

"Miss Miranda," Winston could only go on repeating when she was inside.

"Go and get me a bathrobe or something, Winston. For pity's sake." She scolded with her eyes.

Winston stood on for a minute more, trying to keep his gaze only on her face.

She could hear him mumbling and making other silly sounds as he went upstairs.

Pearl Miranda lowered the shade for the picture window, and then seeing the shade up on a smaller side window, she lowered it also. She picked up a music album and held this over her.

"For God Almighty's sake," Winston said when he handed her a bathrobe.

She put it on with some difficulty, and Winston did not help her. She sat down.

"What can I get for you?" he wondered.

"Usually they give people brandy in such cases," Miss Miranda said. "Cases of exposure," she spoke with her usual precise culture and refinement. "But I think you remember my views on drinking."

"I don't drink either, Miss Miranda," Winston told her.

"Some hot milk might be all right." She seemed to speak condescendingly now. "In case of a chill coming on." Looking down at her bare feet, she inquired, "Do you have any house slippers, by chance."

"I have some that were my mother's," Winston told her.

That will be fine she was about to say, but he was already racing up the steps.

When he came back, he acted a bit more like himself, and he helped her on with the tickly, rabbit-lined house slippers.

"What happened to you?" he asked, looking up at her from his kneeling posture before her.

"Get me the hot milk first," she told him.

He turned to go out into the kitchen, then wheeling around he said: "Miss Miranda, are you really all right?"

She nodded.

"Shouldn't I call the doctor?"

She shook her head vigorously.

He came back into the room, his left hand slowly stealing up to his throat. "You were assaulted, weren't you?" he asked.

"No, Winston, I was not," she replied. "Now please fix me my milk." She spoke to him much as she would have twenty years ago in her classroom.

Miss Miranda sank back into the warmth and mild comfort of the bathrobe and slippers while he was in the kitchen. She could hear him muttering to himself out there as he went about the task of warming the milk. She supposed all lonely people muttered to themselves, and it was one of the regrettable habits she could never break in herself.

Waiting, she looked at his Baldwin piano loaded with Czerny practice books. Another stack of music books sat on his piano stool.

She felt depressed thinking of Winston earning his living sitting all day and part of the evening hearing ungifted children play scales. It was not a job for a man.

Then she thought of how her own sister had felt sorry for her having to teach the eighth grade.

"I'm shaking more now than when you walked in," Winston mumbled inaudibly, bringing in a little Mexican tray with a steaming pot of milk and a cup.

"Doesn't that look nice," Miss Miranda said.

"I'll get you a napkin, too." And he left the room again.

"Don't bother," Miss Miranda called out after him, but not vigorously, for she wanted a napkin.

She hiccuped a bit drinking the hot milk.

Winston cleared the exercise books from the piano stool, sat down and watched her drink the milk.

"Just a touch of cinnamon maybe?" He pointed to her cup.

She shook her head.

"I just took a pie out of the oven a couple of hours ago," he informed her. "Would you like a piece?"

"What flavor is it, Winston?" Miss Miranda wondered.

"Red raspberry," he told her. "Fresh ones."

She studied his face a second. "I might at that," she spoke as if consulting with a third party.

"Do you do all your own cooking, Winston?"

"Since Mother died, yes," he said. "But even in her day I did quite a bit, you know."

"I bet you're a good cook, Winston. You were always a capable boy." Her voice lowered as she said the second sentence.

"I haven't really talked to you since the eighth grade," Winston reminded her in a rather loud voice.

"I expect not." Miss Miranda drank some more of the milk. "My, that hits the spot."

"Wouldn't you like another hot cup?"

"Yes, I think I would," she replied.

He took the tray and all and went out into the kitchen.

Miss Miranda muttered when he had gone, and held her head in her hands, and then suddenly, as if in pain, she cried out, "God!"

Then she straightened out her face and got calm, her hands folded on her bathrobe, for Winston's return.

He handed her a new cup of milk, and she thanked him.

"You're not hurt now, Miss Miranda," he ventured again. He looked very scared.

"I've had a trick played on me is all, Winston." She opened her eyes at him wide.

Somehow, however, she did not seem to be telling the truth, and as she did not look away, Winston looked down at the floor, an expression of sorrow and disappointment about his mouth and eyes. Then he got up from the piano stool and went over to an easy chair and plumped himself down.

"You gave me a start." He put his hand across his chest.

"Now don't you give out on me," she said.

"You don't want me to call the police or anybody?" he asked, and she could see how upset he was getting.

"Just calm down, now. Of course I don't want the police. We'll handle this our own way."

"You said it was a joke, Miss Miranda."

She nodded.

There was a long silence.

"Ready for your raspberry pie?" he asked weakly.

She wiped her hands carefully on the linen napkin. "You could have just given me a paper napkin, Winston," she told him. "Do you have to do your own laundry, too?"

He mumbled something which sounded like *I'm afraid I do.* "I'll get you that pie." He went out of the room.

He came back, after rather a lengthy absence, with a generous piece of red raspberry pie on a hand-painted plate.

"A pretty, pretty sight," Miss Miranda said.

She bit into her piece of pie and said *Mmm.*

"I wish you would let me do something for you," he almost whined.

"Now sit down, Winston, and be quiet. Better do nothing than do the wrong thing," she admonished.

"I know you haven't done anything wrong, of course," Winston said, and his voice sounded prophetic of weeping.

"Now, I'll explain everything just as soon as I have eaten your pie here," she told him. "But it's all nothing to be concerned about."

"Did anybody see you come in here?" he wondered.

She chewed on for a few seconds. "I suspect they may have. Who lives across the street from you there?" She pointed with her fork in the direction of the house in question.

"Not Bertha Wilson," Winston exclaimed.

"A woman came out on that porch. I think she saw me. Of course I know Bertha Wilson," Miss Miranda said.

"Oh, gosh." Winston raised his voice. He looked at her now almost accusingly. "It's all so unusual," he cried, thinking something much more extreme than his words gave inkling of.

"Winston, you've got to keep calm," Miss Miranda told him. "I *had* to come in here tonight. You know that."

"I don't begrudge you coming in here," he said, and he was more in possession of himself.

"Then let's both be calm and collected." She handed him the empty pie plate. "What beautiful work people did when they painted their own china." She nodded at the plate.

"My Aunt Lois hand-painted all of Mother's china."

He left the room with the plate, and there was complete silence everywhere for a few minutes. Then she heard the water running in the kitchen, and she realized he was doing the dishes.

"He's a neat one," she said out loud.

She shook her head then, though she did this about something else than his neatness, and she cried, "God!" again.

In about a quarter of an hour, he came on back into the living room, sat down, crossed his legs, and said, "Now."

"I don't think I'm even going to have a chill." She smiled at him.

Winston was looking at her narrowly, and she thought he was less sympathetic. There was a look of irritability on his face. His mouth had set.

"How long has it been since you lost your mother?" Miss Miranda said.

"Two years this April," he replied without expression. Miss Miranda shook her head. She opened the linen napkin out and put it over the lap of the bathrobe.

"What happened tonight was a joke," she said, and stopped.

"Did many people see you cross over the school playground?" he wondered.

"The school playground?"

"There are the fewest trees there to hide under," he explained.

"I couldn't tell if anybody saw me or not," she said.

"Miss Miranda, if you were . . . *harmed,* you must have me call the doctor."

"You want me to leave?" she inquired. "I will—"

"I didn't mean leave," he protested.

"Please be calm, Winston," she asked him.

"I am calm, Miss Miranda. . . . But gosh almighty, nobody can just sit here and act like nothing happened to you. . . . I never heard of such a thing as tonight!"

She sat thinking how it all must seem to him. At the height of her predicament she had not had time to think.

"I'm unhurt, Winston, except for the exposure, and I told you I can see I'm not going to have a chill."

"I can go over to your house and get your clothes."

She nodded pleasantly. "Tomorrow," she said.

"Tonight!" He was emphatic.

"This young man who looked like one of my own former students came into my classroom at six o'clock tonight," she began her story. "I was cleaning the blackboard."

Winston watched her, his face drained of blood.

"He asked me if I remembered him, and I said I didn't, though his face was familiar. . . . He then asked if I remembered Alice Rodgers. Of course, I remembered her. We just expelled her last term, you know. She had gotten herself and nearly every boy in the eighth grade in all that trouble. You remember reading about it all in the paper . . ."

"Do you remember all that about Alice Rodgers?" Miss Miranda asked him.

Winston half-nodded.

"This young man, oh, he couldn't have been more than twenty . . . certainly not more than your age at the most, Winston . . . he said, 'I think you ought to have to pay for what you did to Alice Rodgers, ruining her name and reputation.'

" 'I only wanted to make a real future for Alice Rodgers,' I told him.

" 'In the reformatory?' he asked with an ugly grin."

Miss Miranda stopped, perhaps expecting Winston to help her on, but he did nothing.

"Then," Miss Miranda said, "he asked me to take off my clothes. He had a gun, you see."

Winston got up and walked in the direction of the next room.

"Where are you going?" Miss Miranda cried.

He looked back at her, asked her to excuse him, and then came back and sat down.

"He said he would use the gun if I didn't do exactly as he said," she spoke in a matter-of-fact tone.

Miss Miranda was looking at Winston, for she was certain that he was not listening to what she said.

"He took all my clothes away from me, including my shoes, and keys, and then, saying he hoped I would remember Alice Rodgers for the rest of all our lives, he walked out, leaving me to my plight. . . ."

Winston was looking down at the carpet again.

Miss Miranda's voice continued: "I called out to him from the bannister to come back. 'How will I get home?' I called after him."

Her voice now trailed off. Suddenly she held her head in her hands and cried, "Oh, God! God!"

"Are you in pain?" Winston looked up sleepily from the carpet.

"No," Miss Miranda replied quickly.

"My head's in a whirl," Winston told her.

"I don't remember that young man at all," Miss Miranda went on. "But you know, Winston, after you've taught so many years, and when you're as old as I am, all young people, all old people, too, look so much alike."

"Miss Miranda, let me call somebody! We should inform—"

"No," she told him. "I won't hear of it. Now, please be calm and don't let what has happened upset you. I want to stay here tonight."

"This young man you describe. He didn't harm you in any way?"

"He did not," Miss Miranda said in the voice of one who defends.

She looked at Winston.

Without warning, he began to gag. He rushed out of the parlor to a small room near the kitchen.

He evidently did not have time to close the door behind him. She could hear him vomiting.

"Oh, dear," Miss Miranda said.

She came into the bathroom and watched him. He was straining very hard over the toilet bowl.

"Winston, I am going to hold your head," she advised him. He made no motion.

She held his head while he vomited some more.

When he had stopped, she took a fresh wash cloth off the rack, and wiped his mouth.

"I've had the virus," he explained.

Suddenly he turned to the bowl again and vomited.

"Poor lad," she said, wiping his mouth again with the cloth.

"You must lie down now," she admonished him.

He walked toward an adjoining room where there was a double bed, and lay down on it.

She helped him off with his shoes, and put the covers partly over him.

"I'm afraid it was me who upset you," she apologized.

"No, Miss Miranda, it's the virus. Can't seem to shake it off. I catch it off and on from my pupils. First from one, then the other."

"Just rest quietly," she said.

When he had dozed off, she exclaimed again, "God! God!"

She must have dozed off, too, in her chair by the double bed, for some time later she awoke with a start and heard him vomiting again in the bathroom, and she hurried in to hold his head.

"Winston, poor lad," she said, feeling his hair wet with sweat.

"How could you stand to watch me be sick like that," he wondered later when they were back in the bedroom.

"I've taught public school for thirty years," she reminded him.

"Miss Miranda," he said suddenly, "you were raped tonight, weren't you?"

She stared at him.

"You've got to let me call the doctor." He wiped his mouth.

"I was not . . . raped," she denied his statement.

He watched her.

"That fellow just asked you to take off your clothes?"

She nodded.

"On account of Alice Rodgers." He echoed her story.

"I had testified against Alice in court," she added, "and they sent her to the reformatory."

"Well, if it's your story," he said.

"I wouldn't lie to you," Miss Miranda said.

"Nobody will believe you," he told her.

"Aren't you talking too much, Winston?" Miss Miranda showed concern for his health.

He did not answer.

"Bertha Wilson saw you across the street," he said sleepily.

"She was looking in my direction all right," Miss Miranda admitted.

"She must have seen you then."

"Oh, it was quite dark, Winston, after all."

"Bertha's got real X-ray eyes."

"Well, so she saw me," Miss Miranda said. "I had to come in somewhere."

"Oh, it's all right," Winston said. "Nobody will think anything about *us*."

"Oh God!" Miss Miranda cried suddenly.

Winston raised himself on his elbows.

"You in pain, Miss Miranda? Physical pain?"

She stifled back her sobs.

"Miss Miranda," Winston began. "That young man that came into your classroom tonight . . . are you listening to me . . . that young man was Fred Rodgers. Alice Rodgers' older brother."

Miss Miranda went on making the stifling sounds.

"Did you hear what I said, Miss Miranda?"

She nodded.

"Alice Rodgers' older brother," he repeated. "I know him. Listen, Miss Miranda, I know he wouldn't stop at just taking away your clothes. Don't you think I have any sense at all?"

He looked away from the look she gave him then.

"Knowing Fred Rodgers the way I do, Miss Miranda, I know he wouldn't stop at what you said he did. He had it in for you for sending his sister to the reform school."

"I'm nearly sixty years old, Winston," Miss Miranda said in the pool of darkness that was her chair. "I'd rather we didn't talk about it, if you don't mind."

"You've got to call the doctor," he said.

Miss Miranda looked down at the long lapel of her bathrobe.

"You had blood on you, too," Winston told her.

A moment later, he screamed and doubled up with pain in the bed.

"Winston, for pity's sake."

"I think I got an attack of appendicitis," he groaned. "Ouch, ouch, ouch." He touched his stomach.

"Do you want a doctor then?" she cried, as if he had betrayed her.

He lay back in the bed and groaned. His face went a kind of green, then yellow, as if suddenly illuminated by a searchlight.

"Dear God. God!" Miss Miranda cried.

"I may get all right," Winston told her, and he smiled encouragement at her from out of his own distress.

"Oh, what shall I do. What *shall* I do," she cried.

"I guess we both will have to have the doctor," Winston told her.

"I can't tell him, Winston. . . . I'm sixty years old."

"Well, you let *him* do the worrying now, Miss Miranda."

"You knew this Fred Rodgers?" She cried a little now. Winston nodded.

"I never taught him, though." She sighed. Suddenly she cried again, "Dear God. God!"

"You try to be calm, Miss Miranda," he comforted her.
He seemed almost calm now himself.

"Why don't you lay your head down on the bed, you look so bad," he told her.

"Oh, aren't we in the worst situation, Winston," she said.

She cried a little.

She laid her head down on the bed, and he patted her hair a moment.

"I don't know how many people saw me," she said.

Winston lay back, easier now. His pain had quit.

Miss Miranda, suddenly, as if in response to his pain's easing, began to tremble violently.

"Get into bed," he told her. "You've got a chill coming on."

He helped her under the covers.

She screamed suddenly as he put her head down on the pillow.

"Just try to get as quiet as possible, Miss Miranda." He helped her cover up.

She was trembling now all over, crying, "Oh, God! At sixty!"

"If you can just get a good night's rest," he comforted her.

"Dear God. Oh, God!"

"In the morning the doctor will fix you up."

"I can never go back and teach those children," she said.

Winston patted her hand. His nausea had left him, but he had a severe headache that throbbed over his temples.

"What is that woman's name across the street again?" Miss Miranda questioned him.

"You mean Bertha Wilson."

Miss Miranda nodded.

"I taught her in the eighth grade. Way back in 1930, just think."

"I wouldn't think about it, Miss Miranda."

"Wouldn't think about what?"

"Anything."

"I can't believe this has happened," she told Winston.

"The doctor will come and fix us both up."

"I don't see how I can have the doctor or go back to school or anything," she wept.

She began crying hard now, and then after a while she got quiet.

"Go to sleep," he said.

He had thought to go upstairs and sleep in the bedroom that had been his mother's, but he didn't know whether he had the strength to get up there, and in the end he had crawled back under the covers next to Miss Miranda, and they both lay there close to one another, and they both muttered to themselves in the darkness as if they were separated by different rooms from one another.

"Good night," he said to her.

She looked up from her pillow for a moment.

"Good night, sweetheart," he said again, in a much lower voice.

She looked at the wall against which he had said the last words. There was a picture of his mother there, pretty much as Miss Miranda remembered her.

"God," Miss Miranda whispered. "Dear God."

Plays

Children Is All

SCENE I

It is the afternoon before the Fourth of July in a small town near Cairo, Illinois. The day is warm, but not oppressively so. In the near distance one can hear the sound of exploding firecrackers, and further off a military band. From the house nextdoor, at irregular intervals, one hears a trumpet blown by the lips of an amateur.

Edna Cartwright, 50, and Leona Khetchum, 60, are sitting in their straight-back chairs in the parlor of Edna's white frame house.

LEONA

I can't believe today's the day for Billy to come, Edna.

EDNA

I didn't sleep a wink all night thinking about it, and then when it was time to get up, my eyelids seemed glued on . . . No, I can't believe he's coming . . . today.

LEONA

And all night long the firecrackers going off, we wouldn't have been able to sleep in any case! . . . And in the middle of the night, I suddenly remember now, I thought I heard voices in argument. . . .

EDNA

Voices?

LEONA

I could have sworn . . . then about 5 A.M., that silly child of a Hilda begun practising on her trumpet.

EDNA

I heard her . . . Small wonder I could hardly bend over to get into my house-slippers this morning.

LEONA

But those voices in the night arguing and talking . . . was as real to me as. . . .

EDNA

About half-past two this morning I thought I heard Billy call to me. . . .

LEONA

Edna!

EDNA

You know I don't often imagine things. But I could have sworn before a judge he spoke to me. Then I laid awake listening to the courthouse clock strike every blessed hour . . . And your firecrackers, Leona . . . You must have heard me call out to him is all.

LEONA

It was a nightmare then, Edna. . . .

EDNA

No, I wasn't asleep at the time . . . Oh, that look of surprise on your face, Leona! It's priceless. I can't help laughing.

LEONA

The only reason I showed any surprise, dear, is because
it's you who said you thought you heard somebody that
wasn't there . . . You're such a skeptical person, Edna.
There's very little superstition in you, goodness knows.
And when *you* say that Billy called you . . . well . . . .

EDNA

There's no superstition in me, Leona, and no religion.
Why say there is? . . . Pastor Stover has worn out three or
four pair of shoes paying his calls on me. A waste of shoe
leather. I've never been inside his church since he took up
his duties here five years ago, and I don't suppose I ever
will now . . . Sometimes, though, I think I do believe in
a kind of a thing like thought transference . . . There's
something about it . . . When Billy was little, he and I used
to play a game at which we guessed one another's thoughts
. . . Oh, it was only play . . . But I can still hear him say,
"Mom, I can send thoughts to you!" . . . Your imagination
works overtime.

LEONA
(mending a tablecloth)
What did Billy call out to you . . . while you were sleeping
last night?

EDNA
I told you I wasn't sleeping at the time.

LEONA
Do you remember any of his words?

EDNA
Yes. He called to me in the awfullest worried voice, like
once when he was a little boy and got his head cut open
. . . Oh it looked worse than it was, but there was so much
blood . . . I had to clean the wound right on the spot . . .

Didn't have any water or iodine or anything . . . I just used my own . . . (*She puts her handkerchief to her mouth and moistens it absentmindedly.*) . . . well, never mind what I used. But last night, I thought I heard his voice call something like, "Mom . . . Mother . . . Be sure to recognize me now when I come home today, hear? Make out you know me when I come home." I raised up in bed then and answered just as if it was real, "But Billy, how wouldn't I know my own flesh and blood."

LEONA

That's what I must have heard then in the night, Edna . . . Your voice.

EDNA

Of course there was nobody there.

LEONA

We have often talked about whether we would recognize Billy if we met him unexpectedly on the street or in a store somewhere.

EDNA

Heavens knows, it's been on my mind. But I'll know him when I see him, Leona, and you will, too, though he's been in that place—been in the State pen—I will use the word like I wasn't ashamed of it—he's been in the penitentiary now nearly fifteen years. You didn't know me as well then. When they took him away, Leona, remember, he was only a boy, not more than eighteen when he was sent up, for God's sake.

LEONA

Think of a young one that age being sent up!

EDNA

And the few times I got my courage up to pay him a visit —once I got clear up to the prison gates—I couldn't go through with it! Oh I felt so bad to be such a weak thing. But I couldn't go past the iron gates . . . I felt if I went in, I would drop dead . . . Do you realize, Leona, I've never laid eyes on him all these fifteen years?

LEONA

I thought you saw him that one time, dear.

EDNA

You're mistaken. Oh, I went down there often enough. For years, regularly, winter, summer, rain or shine, I took the old Illinois Central—all the way to the pen—like I lived on the road, but I never went past the gates. Maybe I lied once and told you I went in, it preyed so on my mind . . . But the truth is I never did . . . I'm a pretty poor excuse for a mother . . . And all the baked goods, pies and cookies and candy I sent him, you know, the presents and favors— he never acknowledged them. It was his way of showing me his resentment. He paid me back in silence for not visiting him, until this postcard came (*She takes a card from her apron pocket.*) two or three days ago now, written with a pencil stub, telling me he was coming home today.

LEONA

Pardoned at last!

EDNA

(*fiercely*)

Pardoned of course . . . He wouldn't be coming home otherwise. (*angrily*) You know that!

LEONA

Of course, Edna! . . . And he'll make up everything to you now.

EDNA

We'll see . . . But all between that quiet summer day when they took him, to now, fifteen years later, a summer day

again, is one long empty space . . . I found out what kind
of work they put him to in the pen. It was clerical work
of some kind on account of he had been in the First National Bank, I suppose . . . I don't know whether you remember Billy too well or not.

LEONA

I remember him as clear as anything.

EDNA

I often wonder how they treated him in the pen . . . There
was those rumors a few years back he tried to escape . . .
And what's he done all this while for companionship or
fun, I wonder. Has he been blue all the time, or gay and
cheerful some of the while. He never said. He never wrote.
I never knew . . . He paid me back in silence . . . He was
just in that big old gray house of steel and cement, and
his poor-excuse of a mother never went to see him. . . .

LEONA

That's all water under the bridge now, Edna.

EDNA

It is, and I'll brace up now . . . But I never believed Billy
was as guilty as everybody made out at his trial . . . Think
how long ago that was! I can see his white face as he stood
up at the very end of the trial, and his blue serge suit he
had bought just a short few weeks before, I suppose with
the money he took from the bank. . . .

LEONA

Edna!

EDNA

He stole, Leona . . . My boy stole.

LEONA

I don't think anybody thought he was guilty of anything too terrible, Edna. Misled's more the word. Old Judge Graber and the president of the First National Bank were the real culprits. They put Billy up to what he did, and I'll always say it. Then when he got caught, they lit out . . . Of course the president paid for his wrongdoing . . . But if it hadn't been for those two mature men, Billy would never have touched a cent of money that didn't belong to him.

EDNA

You remember more than I do about it . . . Oh, I never knew all the charges against Billy, or what he did exactly . . . But he did wrong! He and I never exchanged a word about it. The trial was so confused . . . And I was so ashamed of myself that I didn't stay in court for the whole of it. Billy asked me to stay, so I would know the story, so he wouldn't be all alone with just accusers . . . I fainted outside the witness room, and was picked up and taken downstairs . . . When I come to, I saw I had soiled my dress . . . Dr. Lindsay called a car for me to go home in. . . .

LEONA

But when the president of the bank shot himself to death in his garage about a year after the trial and when Judge Graber up and left town, people began to see that your boy wasn't the only one to blame . . . They should have opened up the whole case then.

EDNA

Oh, I suppose . . . Some people from the church did come to see me at the time—Billy's old preacher then, Reverend McIntosh—and he asked me if I didn't want to open up

the whole case . . . But what would I have done for money?
. . . Yes, Billy carried the whole weight of the guilty, whoever was first responsible . . . And such an inexperienced
fellow to have to carry such a thing on top of him . . . Me
being widowed so young, I suppose I didn't guide him as
firm as I should have . . . I'm willing to accept my part of
the blame . . . Once a long long while ago, I remember,
he come home from a dance with a bloody nose and a
shiner, and I looked up at him, and said, "Why, Billy,
what have you been up to coming home like this to me?"
And he said back to me, "Nothin' you would know what
to do about anyhow."

LEONA

Oh, Edna.

EDNA

He was right! . . . I didn't know what to do about him then
or today on his homecoming . . . I married too young.

LEONA

You're too hard on yourself!

EDNA

I may not even know what to do when he walks in today!
Remember he's been in that block of cement for fifteen
years . . . He won't be young—or old . . . What kind of
memories can you bring back from the State pen? He'll
be like somebody come back from another world, another
space!

LEONA

Edna, dear. Don't punish yourself.

EDNA

We'll have to be careful with him, Leona . . . That's all
I mean . . . And I don't know if I can be careful enough
. . . My strength's not what it was.

LEONA

You're only fifty. You're strong!

EDNA

It'll be like walking on eggs all the time with him. What if I say the wrong thing?

LEONA

We'll have to make our mistakes . . . Billy won't expect us to be perfect.

EDNA

What would I have done without you these past years, Leona . . . We're as close now as flesh and blood. We've been through everything together . . . It's over ten years you've been with me . . . Without you, I'd have given up any number of times.

LEONA

And what have you done for me? You've given me a home and something to work for when my own children wouldn't.

EDNA

Don't cry, Leona. We've cried too much over our children . . . Let's be glad from now on . . . Billy's coming home after all this time. Nothing else matters . . . I was thinking how that old Mrs. McBane said to me the other evening, "Don't you feel the disgrace his coming back will bring on you just when it had finally all blown over?" Imagine. Disgrace. Oh, the old thing meant well, she just thought that when Billy would go down the street, people would point and say, "Isn't that the Cartwright boy going down there, the one that used to be in the pen?"

LEONA

Edna!

EDNA

I'd die if I heard anybody say that about him, or to his face.

LEONA

Fifteen years is a long time today, Edna. People have forgotten Billy. A new generation has come up, old people who might have remembered about it the most have died, or moved away. Younger people don't remember things that happened before their time . . . Worse things have been committed in this town than anything Billy Cartwright could have done.

EDNA

Amen.

LEONA

Remember Sadie Jeffrey's boy who killed that married woman he had got in trouble when she was going to tell her husband, and they never even caught him? Or Goldie Johnson's oldest daughter when she was found in bed with old Doc Tuttle and he up and died under suspicious circumstances shortly after.

EDNA

Oh, why mention names like that.

LEONA

And remember all the carrying-on at Ed Bagley's hunting and fishing lodge . . . And none of those men are in prison!

EDNA

Let's not go into it anymore, Leona . . . I know it's a pretty shabby little place we live in.

LEONA

Shabby and low-down. My mother used to say to me, "Leona, for a small place like this is, I never saw it fail,

every rotten thing that happens in the country seems to
happen right here first of all."

EDNA

She was right.

LEONA

Everything has happened here. Talk about Chicago! They
won't dare judge Billy too hard.

EDNA

Just the same—

LEONA

(*insistent*)
They won't remember Billy's wrongdoing ... He can make
his way again!

EDNA

You seemed surprised when I told you I had had the woodshed all fixed up, Leona ... Old Mr. Barnes has been out
there working on it off and on for a good six weeks, or
better, and he's not quite done yet, but I never let on to
you what he was doing it for ... I'll tell you now ... You
remember how Billy used to draw and paint and make
little woodcarvings in his spare time? Open that drawer
there in the cabinet and bring out those things there
wrapped in the tissue paper. . . .

(*Leona removes some paint brushes and other artist's
materials from the drawer, and brings them to Edna.*)

EDNA

I've bought him these fine imported brushes and paints
and these carving tools ... You see, I've had Mr. Barnes
make the woodshed into a studio!

LEONA

You don't say so.

EDNA

It's not foolish, is it, Leona ... It's extravagant, I know, like all those things I sent to the pen ... They cost me a good deal.

LEONA

You can't begrudge him expense on a day like this.

EDNA

You are enthusiastic about artist's materials, aren't you, Leona?

LEONA

Of course I am. I was a bit surprised, of course, but only because I hadn't thought about him being an artist. I'm enthusiastic, Edna.

EDNA

Maybe he won't care to be a painter.

LEONA

Of course he will, Edna.

EDNA

I've even put a cot out there in the woodshed ... You know he's been alone a lot in the pen ... Maybe he will like to go out in the woodshed and be by himself to get away from us from time to time. If he don't want to draw and paint, he don't have to, of course. He can do what he wants to.

LEONA

Well, he can't live on air, can he? What will he do to support himself?

EDNA

I wasn't going to come to that for a time, Leona. We can't look at all our problems in the face at once.

LEONA

Of course you're right, darling. Don't you worry about him finding himself, for he will. . . .

EDNA

We'll have to hope and pray he will want to do something. If we lived in a big city, it might be easier for him to find himself again. What you say about the old people in town being dead or gone and the younger people not remembering is only half true, Leona. If one man remembers, pretty soon the whole town will.

LEONA

But people are more forgiving today, Edna, or more indifferent. They won't hold his mistake so much against him as they would have, say, before the last war.

EDNA

I hope you're right . . . Everybody should have their chance to start over.

LEONA

And Billy will find his, you mark my words.

EDNA

Leona, we've got to *give* Billy his chance. He can't just find it.
> (*The sound of a trumpet, blown amateurishly, is heard.*)

LEONA

But, Edna!

EDNA

You heard me. He can't go out and look for his chance and his opportunity. We'll have to bring it to him!
> (*In the silence between the two women which follows, a door is heard opening and closing. Hilda, a girl of 18, comes in, carrying a trumpet in her hand.*)

HILDA

Good afternoon, Edna. Leona.

EDNA

Sometimes you startle the daylights out of me, rushing in here the way you do, Hilda. (*Hilda bends down and kisses Edna.*) You're in the house before a person hears the door opening. Don't knock, scrape your feet, or say how-do-you-do ... But it's all right, dear, because it's you. Anybody else I'd take the broom to. But don't blow your trumpet again today, we've enough ruckus with the firecrackers.

HILDA

Is today the day?

LEONA

Hilda, please. What did I tell you?

EDNA

Sit down, petty. On the footstool here, and try to act like you were a young lady. Put this down. (*She refers to Hilda's trumpet.*) My, how glossy and alive your hair looks today. (*Edna strokes the girl's hair.*) And I don't suppose you even bothered to brush it or put the comb through it.

HILDA

What time is he coming, Edna?

LEONA

I'll be out in the linen room, Edna, if you want me. (*She goes into the back of the house.*)

HILDA

What time is Billy coming home?

EDNA

We don't know for sure.

HILDA

But today is the day, ain't it, Edna . . . I've got it marked down on my calendar.

EDNA

His postcard said today. But he didn't tell what train or plane he would be on . . . It's not as though he was expecting the brass band to meet him, you know. I expect he'll come by bus. I don't think he'd be on a plane.

HILDA

Why ever not?

EDNA

Oh, planes weren't so popular fifteen years ago . . . And then people are more apt to recognize you on a plane, I feel. . . .

HILDA

Oh, Edna, I know Billy don't have any real reason to be ashamed. I know he didn't do anything really bad. Even Uncle Ben says he don't think Billy did anything so serious.

EDNA

(puzzled by Hilda's ardor)

Well, Hilda, we can't begin on that . . . Billy made his mistake and he paid for it. Everybody makes mistakes, but most people don't pay a lot for them. . . . Billy paid heavy.

HILDA

And now he can forget about it. And he has the remodeled woodshed.

EDNA

You know about it!

HILDA

Oh, Edna, of course. I watched from Uncle Ben's porch . . . It's so crazy. I want to go inside and see how you've fixed it up.

EDNA
(*vaguely*)
You'll have a chance by and by.

HILDA
You sound sad for a homecoming, Edna.

EDNA
(*stung*)
I can't afford to be that, Hilda. If I don't do another thing, I can't show what I feel.

HILDA
To Billy?

EDNA
To nobody! I've got to be granite, like that place he's been kept in. I've got to give out hope and gladness, and opportunity all at the same time. Everything he didn't have where he's been I've got to give to him here.

HILDA
I'll help you, Edna.

EDNA
(*laughing deprecatingly, and then petting Hilda*)
I'll need your help, dear . . Because I'm afraid.

HILDA
You're not afraid, Edna. I can't believe you are.

EDNA
You've probably never known fear, Hilda, the real kind. No wonder your hair is so glossy and long . . . But Billy's coming back, and we'll make him content. So there. (*They embrace.*) Now you'll have to go along.

HILDA
You'll give him a wonderful welcome!

EDNA

(*moved*)

Goodbye, dear. We'll call you in a day or so when he's back and settled.

HILDA

Oh, I'll be over before then, Edna ... I'll be watching from the front porch.

EDNA

Goodbye, sweetheart. Leona and I still have tons of work before Billy gets here.

(*Hilda goes out, and in a moment Leona returns.*)

LEONA

The door a-slamming was Hilda, I suppose.

(*The trumpet sounds from outside.*)

EDNA

I'm always about to compare her to a hummingbird until I remember all the noise she makes.

LEONA

She comes in like a bird maybe, but she lands like an avalanche.

EDNA

(*musing*)

She's a bird all right. A little guardian bird.

LEONA

She must have done something to please you today ... Oh, that trumpet splits my ears!

EDNA

I envy her flitting in and out, so carefree and young ... Freedom and youth, they go together.

LEONA

That's about all a child without a father to give her a name can ever have, I expect.

EDNA

Uncle Ben certainly takes no interest in her.

LEONA

And why on earth an old widower like him took a little thing like that out of the Children's Home to bring up beats me. She'd been better left where she was, in the same boat with the other little fatherless bastards.

EDNA

Leona. . . .

LEONA

Well, we're the only ones ever pay any attention to her.

EDNA

That's about all we do give her, attention.

LEONA

You've done a lot for her, Edna, in little ways.

EDNA

She's so excited over Billy's coming. I can't understand it. You'd think he was almost her brother.

LEONA

(*evasive*)

She's looking for affection, anywhere she can find it.

EDNA

Well, it's curiosity in the case of Billy, I suppose.

LEONA

And why not? . . . She's heard talk about Billy for years, as—

EDNA

As the boy who got sent to the pen!

LEONA

I'm sorry, Edna . . . I didn't mean. . . .

EDNA

Don't apologize, for God's sake, not about that.

LEONA

I only meant, a young girl like her regards it all as something romantic!

EDNA

Romantic!

LEONA

Exciting then. No, romantic. It's romantic for a young girl to think about someone coming home from prison.

EDNA

So that's what young girls are romantic about!

LEONA

She's still a child even though she's getting on to be a young lady.

EDNA

I don't see who Billy could interest now but you and me . . . truthfully.

LEONA

(*in a low voice*)
Then somebody's going to have to open their eyes wider.

EDNA

The woodshed excited Hilda so. Because it's to be his, I gather.

LEONA

Oh, Hilda's interested in everything we so much as mention. After all, what is there at Uncle Ben's to interest anybody. Income tax forms, books on rent and mortgages, paperweights, ten pair of magnifying glasses, and an old man's set of spittoons.

EDNA

She couldn't go get interested in a man who's been in prison!

LEONA

For God's sake, Edna . . . The way you look when you say that!

EDNA

I don't minimize what he did, Leona, like some people.

LEONA

Edna, there's something I've been meaning to tell you, though I promised Hilda I never would . . . But I owe you my first allegiance.

EDNA

(hurt and suspicious)

Don't tell me anything if you don't want to.

LEONA

I think I owe it to you . . . It will explain so much too about the way she acts today . . . You've got to know it . . . You can keep it as a secret and she won't know I gave it away.

EDNA

I'm not going to worm it out of you, Leona.

LEONA

You musn't take it to heart, though, Edna . . . You must promise me you won't.

EDNA

It was your idea to tell me, now tell me.

LEONA

Hilda's been visiting Billy in the pen, Edna.

EDNA

That's not true!

LEONA

Since a year ago.

EDNA

That can't be, Leona ... She couldn't never get there and back by herself.

LEONA

Uncle Ben drove her.

EDNA

She visited Billy ... What a low-down sneaking trick.

LEONA

She only wanted to because she thought it was the right thing!

EDNA

A little illegitimate nobody like that thinks she can teach me my duty!

LEONA

She'd be sorry if she knew it hurt you ... She didn't want to do that. ...

EDNA

(*somewhat appeased*)

No, of course she didn't. (*coldly calm*) You did right to tell me, and now we can forget it, Leona ... We won't mention it to anybody again.

LEONA

That suits me.

EDNA

You did right to tell me . . . How did he receive her—visit?

LEONA

I don't know.

EDNA

Didn't you ask?

LEONA

I guess I was too surprised to . . . No, I told you all she told me . . . Except she was afraid you'd find out. She's so fond of you. We'll wait till she sees him, Edna. We'll know how he received her then.

EDNA

When *she* sees him?

LEONA

Edna—

EDNA

When *we* see him. We don't know what will happen! What if he's all scarred and horrible, Leona. And mean! What if he's cruel!

LEONA

Oh, Edna. Your boy wouldn't be cruel. No matter what they done to him.

EDNA

I pray he won't be. I couldn't bear for him to be . . . But he's been with criminals for fifteen years.

LEONA

(*anguished*)
Even if at the first . . . he was, Edna. . . .

EDNA

Yes.

LEONA

Being home with you again would finally change him back.

EDNA

I expect you're right. (*The trumpet sounds, but vaguer, and played more execrably than usual.*) I expect so. (*There is the sound of a car drawing up near the house.*)

EDNA

Leona, is that somebody stopping their car out in front?

LEONA

I just have my reading glasses on, dear.

(*A firecracker goes off outside.*)

EDNA

Oh that hideous sound. I . . . Don't tell me that's Reverend Stover sitting in that parked car out there. (*She goes to the window.*)

LEONA

It's his old beat-up Buick all right . . . He's just parked, dear, he wouldn't be coming in.

EDNA

Reverend Stover never knew Billy. Reverend McIntosh was our pastor when Billy was to home . . . You don't suppose Reverend Stover knows today's the day, Leona?

LEONA

I'm afraid word has gone round.

EDNA

Well, you can't keep a secret like that, Leona. It's not to be expected.

LEONA

He's coming in!

(*Reverend Stover pulls on the front doorbell. He is a man of about 35, lean and athletic in appearance, not like the common notion of a small-town preacher. His clothes are severe but not clerical, and he wears a straw hat.*)

STOVER

Mrs. Cartwright, good day. May I come in for just a moment?

EDNA

By all means. Of course, Reverend. I was just saying to Leona, I'll bet you that's Pastor Stover parking his car by the walk as sure as day.

STOVER

I had some calls around the neighborhood and thought I'd drop by to see how you and Miss Khetchum were getting along.

EDNA

Old ladies like us have to get on, Reverend, one way or another. Nobody would put up with us if we didn't. Sit down, please, right over there, if you will. Can't Leona bring you some freshly made lemonade? You look warm, Reverend.

STOVER

It is a bit hilly up past the Robertsons', all the way up ... I have to make up my mind always which can take the incline better, my car or me.

LEONA

I'll bring the Reverend a cool glass of lemonade. (*She begins to leave.*)

STOVER

Instead of the lemonade, would it be too imposing on you ladies' hospitality if I asked for a cup of Leona's good hot coffee?

LEONA

Hot coffee, Reverend?

EDNA

Of course, Leona . . . Iced coffee is about as flat as lemonade . . . And I remember how the Reverend flattered you, Leona, about your coffee the last time he was here . . . Make it a little strong. And bring out the fresh banana cake, dear, wrapped up in the cloth on top of the china closet. (*Leona goes into the kitchen.*) And the linen napkins too, dear, don't forget!

STOVER

Oh now you're going to too much trouble. (*Edna stops him with a look.*) What a beautiful part of town you picked out to live in, Mrs. Cartwright. You're really in the country and yet still part of the town.

EDNA

As a matter of fact, we're just outside the city limits by fifty or sixty yards. You pass the sign as you drive out here. That's why they can shoot off the firecrackers. We're just outside the city limits . . . But I didn't pick this location, Reverend. It was all I could find at the time.

STOVER

All I know is that this is the pleasantest house I come to.

(*The trumpet sounds.*)

EDNA

I didn't intend to be so much like a hermit when I moved out here, but the town began growing in the other direction, you see, and it's kept going that way ever since. I can't say I'm too sorry. Except for the firecrackers and the trumpets!

STOVER

I hope my dropping in just now hasn't inconvenienced you.

EDNA

It's done just the opposite, Reverend.

(*Hilda enters as the Reverend Stover and Mrs. Cartwright talk; then startled by the presence of a visitor, she is about to run off.*)

EDNA

There you are again, Hilda. (*somewhat harshly*) We heard you on the trumpet, warning us, I guess, of your arrival, dear. Now what is it? Well, come in, my dear, and say how-do-you-do to Reverend Stover, even though you don't go to his church.

STOVER

Hello, Hilda. You'll excuse an old man not getting up to greet you ... Your hair gets more beautiful each time I see you. What's your secret?

EDNA

(*somewhat drily*)
Youth, I'm afraid, Reverend.

STOVER

I won't dispute the point with you, Mrs. Cartwright ... Sit down here, Hilda, beside me, and perhaps our hostess may decide to give you a piece of cake.

HILDA

I came to ask a favor of Edna here, and didn't mean to interrupt your talk, Reverend Stover.

EDNA

Sit down, child. You've already interrupted our talk, and you could certainly stand with a piece of cake, I agree. You're all skin and bones under your beautiful hair. (*She pats her.*)

HILDA

No, I only came to ask—

EDNA

You're too thin, dear . . . What did you come to ask?

(*Leona enters with the cake and coffee, and begins serving.*)

HILDA

What was I going to say! You've all paid so much attention to me, I've forgotten . . . Oh, it'll keep for another time.

STOVER

I'll bet somebody is not used to talking in front of the preacher.

HILDA

No, sir, it was only about the woodshed.

EDNA

(*icily*)
Yes, dear.

HILDA

I was thinking . . . (*to Leona, as she takes cake and coffee*) Thank you, Leona . . . I was thinking, do you want to let me arrange some flowers from Uncle Ben's backyard and put them in the woodshed in honor of Billy's homecoming today. It's not too late you know.

(*Leona goes out again.*)

STOVER

(*standing up*)

Billy's homecoming, Mrs. Cartwright! You never told—

EDNA

(*unaware of Reverend Stover's addressing her, gazing fixedly at Hilda*)

Yes, dear, if it will make you happy, of course.

HILDA

But I want it to be what you want, Edna, dear. And what Billy wants.

STOVER

Mrs. Cartwright, please forgive me, sitting here drinking coffee and eating cake ... I had no idea. ... (*He stops, seeing Edna has not heard him.*)

EDNA

We won't know what Billy will want, Hilda ... But go ahead and fix up the place with some of Uncle Ben's flowers. He has some beauties. His tea roses are choice. Make your own kind of place out of the woodshed if you will ... I admit I hadn't thought of flowers.

(*Leona comes back into the room.*)

LEONA

Your Uncle Ben's calling you, Hilda.

HILDA

I can't believe it ... Must be the first time he ever called me since I ... since I came to stay with him.

LEONA

Well, he's calling now out on the front porch, so you better run on home now and find out what he wants ... And don't come back, dear, until tomorrow. We've got our hands full today.

HILDA

Imagine Uncle Ben coming clear out on the front porch to call me. (*She finishes eating her cake.*) Goodbye, Edna . . . Pleased to see you, too, Reverend Stover . . . Bye, Leona.

EDNA

Run along, dear.

STOVER

You must come to see me some time . . . in church, Hilda.

HILDA

Goodbye, all.

STOVER

(*beginning again*)
Mrs. Cartwright!

EDNA

(*still bemused*)
That is odd, old Ben calling to the child from the front porch, Leona. He could have come over instead of shouting his head off. Usually he never cares how long she stays. Is glad to be rid of her.

LEONA

(*firm, almost vindictive*)
Ben thinks Billy's home, Edna. That's why he called her . . . And Reverend Stover's been trying to say something to you for the past ten minutes.

STOVER

(*smiling, nodding*)
Thanks, Leona . . . Mrs. Cartwright, I was completely in the dark about Billy coming home today . . . I hadn't even heard he was pardoned. Had I known, I assure you, I would never have intruded like this.

EDNA

Don't ever say you intruded, Reverend. I'm happy you
came. But I supposed of course when I saw you, you had
come because of Billy...Which would have been only
natural.

STOVER

Good heavens! I'd never have come in like this on his
homecoming. (*awkward*) It is an intrusion...But I'm so
happy he'll be with us again.

(*In Edna's abstraction, he takes up his straw hat.*)

EDNA
(*with great intensity*)
Don't go, Reverend. I'm relieved you're here. Finish your
coffee and cake, why don't you.

LEONA

You've come at the very right time, if you ask me, Reverend.

EDNA

Leona means we're both unsure of ourselves...And we
suppose Billy will be unsure of himself, too. He doesn't
know how he'll find us. We don't know how we'll find him.

LEONA

The plain truth is, Reverend, we're afraid.

EDNA

We're afraid Billy will catch our fear, and that we'll spoil
his welcome. We only want him to feel at home. That's
all. But we don't know if we'll be able to pass the test.

STOVER
(*putting down his hat*)
The test?

EDNA

The test of us making him feel welcome.

STOVER

You will. Believe me. You'll be able to make him realize he's come home at last.

EDNA

You see, he's never written me hardly a line till a few days ago this postcard came (*She takes out the postcard.*) telling us he would be home before the Fourth, for sure, and signed Billy. . . . (*The pastor examines the postcard, then hands it back to Edna.*) All we want to do for him, of course, is make him feel welcome. If we can only bring home to him that we want him here . . . after so many years, and so much silence. . . .

STOVER

Perhaps you will let me ask you one question. . . . (*He braces himself.*) I don't know if you will thank me for asking it or not. If not, feel free to ignore it.

EDNA

I don't know why you'd think I wouldn't let you ask me a question, Reverend. After all, you're my pastor, though I'm not much of a churchgoer, I confess.

STOVER

Thank you for calling me your pastor, Mrs. Cartwright. I need every one of my congregation, and it's the women, the mothers especially, I count on . . . But sometimes a question, just the same, put with the kindest intent, offends or wounds the sensibilities.

EDNA

I'm sure you would never offend me, Reverend.

STOVER

(*thundering*)

Mrs. Cartwright, are you really happy Billy is coming home?

EDNA

Am I what?

STOVER

(*softer, but stern*)

It's so important you answer the question.

EDNA

I see . . . perhaps what you meant about wounding and offending.

STOVER

Don't feel you must answer me, Mrs. Cartwright. I'm only here to help you, and you don't have to say a thing in reply.

EDNA

I've searched myself hard with this same question of yours. I've been ashamed at what I found.

STOVER

There's no need to be ashamed.

EDNA

Yes, but there is. I've found myself wanting where I should be strong. I'm deficient, Reverend.

STOVER

We're all deficient, Mrs. Cartwright, and you're being hard on yourself if you think you stand alone in your fault.

EDNA

I'm afraid for Billy to come home!

STOVER

You mustn't be so troubled.

EDNA

Oh, I'm beyond being troubled. I'm in panic. I'm not up to the demands he'll be sure to make. I see it all, I hold on to Leona here, but she's not up to the demands either. We're both deficient. (*She takes Leona's hand.*)

STOVER

When the moment finally arrives, you'll find your strength. It will be given to you, if you ask for it.

EDNA

Oh, that's a comforting thought. I've clutched at straws. At the shadow of straws. I've gone down on my knees and begged for strength—from anywhere. But inside I'm all water. Where the bones should be, and the blood—there's water.

STOVER

You're not unique, Mrs. Cartwright. In the hour of peril and need, we're wanting. It's our nature.

EDNA

But I'm a mother, Reverend. I have no right to feel like any ordinary woman with her troubles. I'm his mother.

STOVER

Because your concern for him is great, strength will be added to your concern, and when the moment comes, you'll find yourself.

EDNA

Oh, that's what I pray for.

STOVER

Strength will come to you if you keep asking for it. Everything comes, Mrs. Cartwright, if we keep asking. And even if it does not, the asking has opened our hearts, like the parched ground opens for rain.

EDNA

The parched ground—

STOVER

If we call, someone always hears. Remember that.

EDNA

Oh, I want to remember that. That's my kind of thought, if only—

STOVER

What?

EDNA

If I could only take the thought from you, as it comes from your lips.

STOVER

Do so, Mrs. Cartwright.

EDNA

What?

STOVER

Take the thought as it comes to you.

EDNA

I can't. I can't. (*She sobs.*) You see how weak I am. I can't accept your thought. All I can think of is I will fail him. He will walk in, and I will say, or show on my face: "*The ex-convict has come home. I've opened my house to shame and disgrace.*"

STOVER

No, you will not say that. (*He puts his fingers on her lips.*) You will say only what your heart tells you. You will not be held by your fear, Mrs. Cartwright.

EDNA

I can't afford to show my fear. My fear is greater than I am.

STOVER

Mrs. Cartwright! Edna!

EDNA

(*rising*)
It masters me by day and night. It seems to engulf all that
I am, wherever I am. It blots out the world when it comes.

STOVER

(*taking hold of her arm*)
Repeat after me, Edna.

EDNA

Pastor.

STOVER

Repeat after me, I will know no fear.

EDNA

"I will know no fear."

STOVER

Great or small.

EDNA

"Great or small."

STOVER

Definite or vague.

EDNA

"Definite or vague."

STOVER

All-embracing or dimly present.

EDNA

"All-embracing or dimly present."

STOVER

My love will be sufficient for all things.

EDNA

"My love will be—" (*She stops.*)

STOVER

Finish the statement.

EDNA

I can't say another word.

STOVER

You must finish. You have no choice.

EDNA

No! Please don't ask me to say any more.

STOVER

I'm not asking you, Edna.

EDNA

(*insanely*)

I can't say another word. When he comes, if he comes, I will be ready.

STOVER

I'll say the words for you.

EDNA

Thank you, no.

STOVER

I mean to say them here and now, Edna.

EDNA

Please don't say any more, Pastor Stover . . . I implore you. You've been very kind . . . And you've seen how fallen by the way I am. (*bitterly*) That should have made your call worthwhile for you as a man of God . . . Thank you for your help . . . Good day.

STOVER

(quietly, passionately)
"My love will be sufficient!"

EDNA

Yes, I know that's it ... "My love will be sufficient!" Oh, Reverend, Reverend, Jesus, God, what shall I do? (*He holds her to prevent her falling.*)

CURTAIN

SCENE II

(It has grown dark in Edna's parlor. Away from the house, in the distance, the woodshed is now more visible than it had been in the earlier scene, suffused as if by a phosphorescent glow. As before Edna and Leona are sitting together, immobile in the twilight. Outside, an occasional explosion of a firecracker is heard.)

EDNA

I didn't visualize Billy coming home in the dark. I thought he would come at high noon somehow, about the time the Reverend got here, with plenty of sunshine pouring down. That's how I pictured it to myself . . . The post-card was so vague *(She takes it out of her dress pocket and looks at it with difficulty.)*

LEONA

He's sure to be along pretty soon . . . And I'm glad I persuaded you to take a bite of food, for it's kept your strength up, if nothing else . . . And when Billy comes, the chicken and the rest will make a nourishing cold supper.

EDNA

There's no more trains or buses after supper time, Leona. Not any more. You know that.

LEONA

He could have hitchhiked . . . Maybe he stayed at some nearby town to break the trip.

(Edna shakes her head slowly. In the distance, a shadow moves across the front of the woodshed. It stops an instant, then seems to merge into the blackness of the coming night.)

148

EDNA

That meal you prepared this evening, Leona.

LEONA

Yes.

EDNA

I never wanted to eat it—it all looked so beautiful. You spent all day on it, just the preparing, I know. In a thousand wonderful meals you've prepared for me, it was the most wonderful . . . I'd like to thank you for myself . . . and for him. I know what went into it. . . .

LEONA

Edna, stop.

EDNA

You pretend it's nothing, but I know different . . . The way you combined the Virginia ham with the chicken, for example . . . And the old-fashioned corn sticks, and Parker House rolls to boot. Talk about killing the fatted calf.

LEONA

If we'd only known what train he was coming in on, one of us, or somebody from the neighborhood could have met him. . . .

EDNA

All we had to go on was the one postcard . . . One thin bent postcard written with a pencil stub.

LEONA

Maybe he got off at some little place nearby, and is coming on foot the rest of the way.

EDNA

I haven't really got over Reverend Stover's talking to me like that, Leona.

(A sound reaches the room from outside.)

LEONA

Edna, did you hear something?

EDNA

(oblivious)

Reverend Stover shook me up. I've never had such an experience with anybody, let alone a preacher, Leona . . . I felt he communicated something to me . . . that's the word . . . as though through another power.

LEONA

I thought you was going to faint just before he put his arms around you, Edna. He thought so, too, I believe, or he wouldn't have held you so tight.

EDNA

No, I didn't feel as if I was going to faint, Leona . . . I felt I had left the room, the world . . . I don't know where I thought I was.

LEONA

Perhaps you'd best have a medical checkup from Dr. Lindsay some day before too long.

EDNA

Oh, you can't call up a doctor every time you come face to face with yourself.

LEONA

We tried to do too much today. And all them interruptions! We done our best, Edna, anyhow. The house never looked better. The icebox and pantry is stuffed full with food for days ahead, for whenever he shows up.

EDNA

Today's over, Leona. He didn't come.

LEONA

It's still early in the evening, Edna, dear. You've got to remember what travel's like nowadays.

EDNA

You said that before.

LEONA

He's finding out what travel's like today, too, after his fifteen years.

EDNA

The day came and went, and no Billy . . . Let's not try to fool ourselves. We're too used to one another's nerves to pretend. We're both disappointed. I won't make any bones about it. And Leona, I was ready! When Pastor Stover left, I knew I could have met Billy. I was ready for him! I could have made him welcome!

LEONA

Edna! God be praised!

EDNA

I could have made him know I loved him.

(There is the slight sound of a door being opened very quietly. A man's figure steps across the threshold and stands in the shadow of the door. Neither of the women notice his entrance or see him.)

EDNA

I could have made him realize the reason I never visited him in the State pen all these years was because I loved him too much. He would have understood, Leona, if he had come home just then. Everything would have been forgiven.

LEONA

Edna, don't let yourself go so, dear.

EDNA

For the first time in my life, Leona, when Pastor Stover talked to me, fear had left me. That's why it seemed I had left the room. I had lost my fear. I was free, Leona. Do you hear? For the first time I was—

LEONA

You got all that from Pastor Stover?

EDNA

I don't know where I got it from. From God. Who knows? I don't even believe in him, but what does it matter. I got the power from somewhere and now—

LEONA

Don't talk any more, Edna. Rest. You'll only wear your-self out, and for nothing you can change anyhow.

(The intruder moves along the wall a step or two, still in the shadow.)

LEONA

Don't you hear something close by every so often, Edna? Some sound? Just now a moment ago, for instance, even closer.

EDNA
(not having heard Leona)
Now I don't believe in anything any more, Leona. Now that Billy didn't show up, I'm afraid all over again.

(Leona goes to the window and looks out.)

EDNA

You hear children setting off firecrackers, or Hilda over at Uncle Ben's banging around. Children is all . . . Come away from the window . . . Are you listening to what I'm saying? My fear has returned! I feel now that I never want to see Billy again!

(The intruder, who is a young man, squats down against the wall now, and lowers his head.)

EDNA

My old feelings all over again. I never want to see him again, that's it. I couldn't stand the shock now. After getting ready once, getting really ready and being made capable of welcoming him. Never again. He had to disappoint me by not coming when I was ready for him. He's always disappointed me. Since he was a small boy. Always late, from the beginning . . . He was born late. Did you know that, Leona? He was born late.

LEONA

Edna, I'm too tired to hear you.

EDNA

Never on time for anything, he was. Always behind and lagging. Why couldn't he have been like other boys? I needed the right kind of son.

LEONA

Maybe God gives us the children we deserve.

EDNA

(after a pause)
Maybe he does . . . But it's you who are worn out, Leona, dear. I don't seem to require sleep any more. This will be my second night awake. Why don't you turn in? I believe today's been harder on you than it has on me. For I had that one moment free from fear when I felt I was soaring.

(The light on Uncle Ben's porch comes on outside the window. The young man rises and moves away so that he will be out of the reflection.)

LEONA

Edna, you've had the real experience today. I can tell by the sight of your face.

EDNA

Let's leave it be now, Leona.

(The light on Uncle Ben's porch goes off.)

LEONA

I hate to leave you when there's all this unrest in the neighborhood tonight.

EDNA

It's just children, Leona. Fourth of July and all. Do go to bed now.

LEONA

Goodnight, dear. *(She kisses her.)*

EDNA

I used to have these feelings before Billy was born, Leona ... Once just a month or so before he came into the world, I felt like I did today ... As though I'd been transported to some other time or place. It was soothing and wonderful, and yet at last upsetting.

LEONA

Could I bring you anything before I go? Some warm milk maybe and just a bit of whiskey.

(Edna shakes her head. The light on Uncle Ben's porch goes on again.)

LEONA

There go the lights again on Uncle Ben's porch. Did you ever! Every few minutes ... off ... on.

EDNA

It's Hilda.

LEONA

At this hour of night?

EDNA

She could get out of bed and down to the front porch quicker than we can raise ourselves from our chairs . . . Goodnight, Leona. Don't tarry a minute longer. Everything's all right. What would I do without you?

LEONA

Don't say that, dear. Today I've felt so utterly helpless where you're concerned . . . and that's where my life is.

EDNA

Goodnight.

(Leona goes to her room. Edna sits quietly by herself for a time. She turns on the radio, which plays some hillbilly number, followed by an announcer speaking in drawling, unintelligible accents. Then the music plays again. Edna dozes, and the young man gets up from his squatting position near the door and approaches her chair. When he comes into the light, it can be seen that there is blood on his shirt and an ugly wound on his temple. He pauses to study Edna carefully.)

THE STRANGER

Edna! *(insistent)* Edna! It's me, Billy . . . Can you hear me? . . . I don't have but a minute, Edna.

EDNA

(wakening, but not speaking for a lengthy time)
I can't see in the dark.

THE STRANGER

It's Billy. I'm back.

EDNA

(confused)
But Billy didn't come.

THE STRANGER

I can't stay, Edna . . . I broke my way out . . . *again*. Busted
out, Edna. Maybe you guessed from the postcard. I didn't
intend to come to you at first . . . You know how many
times I busted out before?

EDNA

I don't know what you're saying.

THE STRANGER

I broke out this time with the most trouble of all. *(touching his head)* I ain't hurt so bad, though. *(Both he and Edna
seem to lapse into unconsciousness, and he has half fallen
on his knees beside her. He begins again with difficulty.)*
I said I didn't get here without difficulty . . . Do you
hear, Edna? But I had to find out if you would recognize
me after all this time. I had to . . . I won't stay, hear? I
didn't come to bother you.

EDNA

I don't know what you mean or who you are.

THE STRANGER

I heard what you said a while ago, Edna . . . Can you hear
me? . . . It always seems so hard to talk to people in the
dark, as though your voice got drowned out without the
light. *(He raises his voice with great effort.)* I couldn't help
hearing what you said awhile ago about me, Edna, to that
old lady. About me always being late.

*(Edna rouses herself, but she seems to be like a person
about to walk in her sleep.)*

EDNA

I don't know what you're doing in my house, but you'll
have to leave before there's trouble or I call out for somebody . . . My son Billy was only a boy *(She stares at him.)*

and you're a man! (*See sees his wound, and lets out a short cry.*) You're all cut up!

THE STRANGER

I told you I broke out . . . Edna, you know who I am. (*desperately*) Don't act out anything now . . . You know I'm Billy . . . I'm not going to stay . . . I only wanted you to recognize me before I go. I don't expect . . . anything more.

EDNA

I'll have to call for help . . . (*He takes hold of her.*) Don't touch me. I'll have to call.

THE STRANGER

Edna! You know it's me.

EDNA

No, no, you're not him. Billy was only a boy.

(*There is the sound of footsteps. The stranger gets up and makes as if to move into the back of the room until he recognizes it is Hilda who has entered. He falls back down on his knees.*)

HILDA

(*at first not seeing the stranger in the room*)
Edna, are you all right? (*She sees and recognizes Billy. He looks at her, and reaches up and touches her hair slowly.*) Billy! What's happened?

EDNA

What do you mean, Billy?

HILDA

Edna, that's who it is!

EDNA

Do you think I wouldn't know my own boy.

HILDA

Edna, look at him please. Look at him only. You must see it's him.

THE STRANGER

Let her be blind! . . . Let her be blind. *(He falls over forward slightly, his head getting closer to Edna's lap.)*

HILDA

(seeing the blood on the stranger)
He's cut and bleeding! *(in horror)* Billy, you're wounded.

EDNA

I can't have someone bleeding here in my house. Do you hear?

HILDA

Edna, we must call for somebody . . . Oh, Billy, Billy, you're cut bad.

EDNA

Somebody wounded and in my house!

HILDA

Look at him, Edna.

EDNA

Look at him! Is a fatherless little bastard like you to teach me my duty? *(catching control of herself)* I'm sorry, Hilda . . . I can't bear to look at such things . . . You see how ill I am already, just your mentioning such a thing to me. *(Suddenly she looks at the stranger.)* Best go call Dr. Lindsay, Hilda, then. And call the Reverend, too—for whoever we've got here.

HILDA

Will they come at this time of night?

EDNA

(gazing dreamily at the stranger)

Yes, if you tell them for me it's the greatest emergency, Hilda.

HILDA

Dr. Lindsay . . . and Reverend Stover.

EDNA

That's right . . . But wait, just before you go, Hilda . . . You know what . . . I could almost say he reminds me of something from a long time ago . . . When Billy was a baby, he so often fell and got hurt. He played too rough I always told him. When he come home *(She draws the head of the stranger toward her lap.)* bruised and cut up, I used to take my pocket handkerchief *(She removes one slowly from her dress, like a somnambulist, and leans over the intruder.)* and I would moisten it with my . . . spit. *(She does so now.)* And I'd wipe away the dirt and blood. *(She cleans the stranger's forehead.)* I'd wipe away the dirt and blood when we wasn't near a place with water . . . That's a deep cut, there . . . You could lay your finger in it.

THE STRANGER

(looking up at Edna)

Edna!

(Edna takes his head in her lap, as Leona enters the room in her dressing-gown.)

LEONA

The firecrackers woke me up, Edna . . . Then I seen you hadn't been to bed. *(She sees the wounded man and Hilda.)* Good God! . . . What is this? Edna, is that Billy?

HILDA

I'll go get help. *(She rushes out.)*

LEONA

What is it, Edna. . . .

EDNA

I told Hilda to tell them it was the greatest emergency . . . I think considering I've never troubled them before, they may come.

LEONA

Edna. *(She looks down.)* Why, it is Billy.

EDNA

This stranger is Billy? Look again.

(Leona weeps because of Edna's reply.)

EDNA

We done everything we could, didn't we, Leona . . . And now we've sent for help.

LEONA

Edna, for God's sake, do you know who you're holding there in your arms?

EDNA

(becoming incoherent)

I'll never last for Billy's next pardon, Leona . . . You can bet on that.

LEONA

Say something reasonable, dear, now . . . And look who you've got there in your lap.

(As Edna is washing the face of the stranger with her handkerchief he stiffens suddenly and dies.)

EDNA

Did he say something? Did you hear him say something?

(Leona draws back in horror and weeps quietly.)

EDNA

Lift yourself up again, sir . . . just for a moment. Your head is so heavy all of a sudden . . . We've got to get him to a bed, Leona. *(to the stranger)* You've come a long way, I can see by the dust on your shoes . . . Whatever you may have to tell us can keep now till morning.

LEONA

Edna, for God's sake. Look who you've got in your lap there. It's Billy . . . *(She examines the stranger for what seems a long time.)* He's gone.

EDNA

Nothing is our fault, Leona . . . What's happened, happened . . . My wanting Billy has passed so peacefully. *(She nurses the dead man on her knees.)* I feel I almost welcomed him home and put him to sleep myself, as calm as if I'd been. . . .

LEONA

My dear, poor friend.

EDNA

I who couldn't have welcomed a stray dog. . . .

HILDA
(returning)
They're coming right away, Edna . . . the doctor . . . and the Reverend . . . I told them it was an emergency.

LEONA

That's Billy himself she's holding there, Hilda. But it's too late. *(Leona and Hilda embrace.)*

EDNA
(touching the face of the stranger)
In just a minute now, sir, we'll have some help.

LEONA

The knot that's held her together all these years is broken
. . . She won't have to know but little from now on. . . .

EDNA

My wanting Billy has passed, Leona . . . I feel so at ease
with this perfect stranger who came in like from nowhere.
For the first time in my life, Leona, I feel so close to my
own son . . . I feel like I did today when Reverend Stover
came, like I'm soaring, soaring!

CURTAIN

Cracks

Nera is seated in a huge chair under a buttonwood tree in her garden. She is 80 years old. A nurse is with her, who, though younger, looks even older. The child is seen upstairs in his cot.

NURSE

You're still reading that special delivery letter that came last night.

NERA

I only look at it occasionally because it's from the last living member of my family, my brother Floyd. His wife writes the letters because he's the one who had the stroke.

NURSE

I know all about it, Nera.

NERA

He communicates everything he feels to her, since he cannot talk, by some kind of telepathic look. She writes me these letters as if he was speaking to me. They're a great comfort.

CHILD

(from upstairs)

I feel the winds from the cracks again blowing.

NERA

Nonsense. It's summer. Go to sleep.

CHILD

(reading from a book)
"Before I was acquainted with life, I felt the zephyrs of death."

NERA

(correcting)
The *cold* zephyrs.

CHILD

(reading)
"I felt the zephyrs of death blowing from the cracks in my surroundings." *(He stops reading.)* I called to somebody about an hour ago.

NURSE

What on earth do you want now?

CHILD

The winds from the cracks.

NERA

He's always quoting from that book. Never says anything on his own. *(scolding)* I told you and I told you. There are no cracks where you are the wind could get through.

CHILD

It's the nurse's doing.

NURSE

I won't tell you to go to sleep again, because I've never told you in any case, and now I say to you: continue to mention whatever you like, for it is not there.

CHILD

The cracks are closing now . . . I'll doze. . . .

NERA

You've kept me waiting, you and the child, as usual, from commenting on my special delivery letter.

NURSE

Those letters all say the same thing. You completed your comments on them a year ago. We won't listen.

NERA

Since my brother Floyd had his stroke he communicates with his wife by looks. Then she writes down what he is thinking and sends his thoughts to me . . . He's the last of my family . . . When he goes I'll have nobody. . . .

NURSE

I have a thousand things to do besides listen to you. My sewing is waiting for me out there.

NERA

You'll do as you're told, you and the child. How dare you speak to a mistress like that? If it weren't summer, I would cry.

NURSE

Very well, then, tell me the contents of your special delivery letter.

NERA

(happy she can tell)

To fill in the background: my brother had all the advantages because he was the right sex. A university education, fraternities, social occasions. He became a distinguished doctor and then he made not one but twenty fortunes . . . There was this small town in Virginia where he owned all the buildings in town and much of the outlying land . . . Farms, barns, rivers, enough to support a regiment on . . . Every two or three weeks he took vacations . . .

While I . . . My husband turned out to be a petty embezzler . . . Left me with a large family to support . . . My mother used to try to intercede with my brother . . . He was always too busy to hear her . . . He allowed her to become a scrubwoman. . . .

NURSE

That was your sister Kate, not your mother.

NERA

Be quiet, it was mother . . . Kate was the organist . . . Can you imagine, our own mother. Once I picked her up from the floor where she was scrubbing . . . "Nera," she said, "don't please feel sorry for me. You're the one has had the bad breaks. I had two good husbands—buried both of them—and now though I have to scrub for a living . . . I remember happiness." *(Nera weeps.)* Wasn't that a terrible thing for her to say to me, her own daughter? She didn't realize how her remark hurt. It was true but she should not have said it . . . I said, "Mother, mother, you shouldn't have to scrub for a living when your own son is a wealthy investor and owns all of Virginia."

CHILD

I hate cracks!

NURSE

So you said last night.

NERA

(to the audience)

That is not my child speaking . . . It's a neighbor's. She left it here one warm summer evening like tonight when the planet Jupiter was so brilliant in the early sky. She never returned. I couldn't send the poor little thing to an institution . . . But something's wrong with it—with him.

CHILD

You could get rid of the cracks if you tried, you old bitch.

NERA

That child is not only ill, he's upset from within. Now my brother is a hopeless invalid, and cannot speak or read . . . He understands television, they say . . . My mother has been dead many, many years . . . Yet she is the only comfort I still have. Only my mother loved me. Nobody ever loved me but her . . . That is why I could not send this little child to an institution . . . He has nobody, and out there. *(She speaks mysteriously, as if frightened, looking into the distance from which later a figure will emerge.)* If he was sent to an institution, who would he have but doctors and nurses . . : Coarse people used to instruments and charts—they look on the body as an interesting mistake . . . No love in the world! *(She cries.)* Yes, the child is right about the cracks.

(The nurse meanwhile has been sewing on a sewing machine in another part of the room.)

NERA

My children all died one right after another, just when they were getting to be a comfort to me, after the long weariness of raising them . . . Just as they was about to be young men and women, all four of them, one right after another died . . . Each one violently. Their insurance has left me somewhat comfortable, but with nothing to think about really except my mother . . . Nurse, what is that thumping sound? The sewing machine? Very well, yes, mend the curtains, and make new ones if you like, too. . .

CHILD

The cracks are closing now . . . Goody.

NERA

Every night that way, he carries on . . . If he couldn't worry about the cracks, there would be something else for him to fret over . . . We have to have troubles in order to speak . . . If everything went along all right, we might remember nothing . . . when it came to get dark.

CHILD

Goodnight, Nera. The cracks have closed.

NERA

Sleep till morning, precious . . . That's right . . . No, nurse will not leave the house until you come down to breakfast . . . We will meet in the grape-arbor and have our bread and hot milk . . . Thank God, it's summer . . . I hate the winter months . . . One gets so cold, and I always think of the dead out there. I wonder what the dead really do? There must be something after that for them . . . There can't be just nothing, even though, as the unbelievers say, there was nothing we can remember from before . . . I'm sure there's more!

CHILD

Do you hear somebody calling? No? Goodnight. I won't call you or nurse again . . . Goodnight and goodnight and goodnight.

(A faint whishing sound—like a weak but prolonged explosion—is heard.)

NERA

The child never said that before . . . Nurse? *(The nurse is asleep.)* No answer . . . Both fell asleep at their place . . . I thought I heard a strange noise after the child spoke . . . Everything rattled inside . . . And now it's so quiet . . . The universe is completely mysterious and yet no longer

so scary as when I was a child and was afraid of cracks . . .
Only I called them ghosts . . . He calls them cracks. He
called them cracks. *(frightened)* Why do I correct myself?
Oh the awful silence. *(She pauses.)* I should have visited
Mother's grave more often in the winter months. That's
when the dead seem so pitiful, when the snow piles high
and the wind rages, and you know everybody, everybody
at last, with no exceptions, is forgotten in death . . . No
exceptions. Even the great are merely remembered as
great dead, for there is nobody to tender them living love
. . . In the end everybody and everything is forgotten.
(Her head falls over.) I must have dozed just then . . . I
must have fallen fast alseep. *(looking out toward the
audience)* I never go to sleep in a bed unless I have to
. . . I'm afraid . . . Usually when I do it's in the daytime
. . . I go and lie down for an hour or two . . . But during
the night of late years, I don't know why, I keep a vigil
. . . I don't know for whom or what.

*(A figure has been standing off to one side all the
time she has said this, watching her. It is apparently
the figure of a young man, but he is too shrouded in
darkness and in his heavy clothing for us to be sure.)*

FIGURE

Don't you know why, Nera?

NERA

My goodness, you startled me—more than the funny explosion.

FIGURE

I'm surprised you heard it since it seems to have had no
effect on you.

NERA

Should it have had?

FIGURE

Well, I dare say so . . . in view of its being the end . . . of everything.

NERA

I'm glad the child went to sleep and the nurse too, though she was supposed to make the curtains tonight . . . But nurse annoys me with all her questions. Why can't she simply make the curtains? Why does she come to me with all the problems of sewing? I've forgotten how to sew, either by hand or machine . . . I never liked sewing. In the days when I was head of a family, I loved to cook. They said my dishes were superb.

FIGURE

That's all over, along with the memory of it.

NERA

Who are you and what are you coming into my garden for at this time of night? I should be frightened but your voice is so kind I know you're that way too . . . Will you be seated?

FIGURE

The end of the world has come and you don't know it.

NERA

Have you experienced some great grief that you speak like this?

FIGURE

No.

NERA

I have suffered nearly all the usual afflictions and bereavements . . . I lost everybody I loved, and now I'm waiting to join them if there is such a thing as an afterlife . . . I'm of two minds about it . . . In the late evening, if I'm comfortably tired and if the sky is beautiful and mild with stars and planets in easy view, I'm sure there must be more ahead . . . But often when I awake in a stiff posture in the morning, and my milk isn't brought to me by nurse, and the child is complaining and crying, I feel there's nothing after this life . . . And yet it's all so without sense that way . . . There has to be more to make this terrible life have meaning . . . It can't stop here, that would be unfair!

FIGURE

But it's all over, dear person

NERA

Again your beautiful voice! One thinks you are singing. No matter what you say . . . Say anything, I pray you.

FIGURE

It's all over.

NERA

You see, even when you say something without any meaning, it's musical and cadenced . . . I used to play the piano and I sang. I sang in our church choir . . . People came from far and near to hear my voice . . . No matter if all I was going to sing that Sabbath was the anthem, the preacher knew we would fill the house. Then I got married and I lost my voice . . . Or rather I didn't want to sing . . . My voice stayed the same . . . I sang to all my children but the last little fellow . . . I never sang to him . . . And you know he needed it the most because all the time I carried him there were worries—my husband deserted me, and then died in Chicago . . . This little child, the last of all my children, prematurely born, never heard me sing to him . . . He passed away when he was three . . . That's why the little boy upstairs reminds me of him.

FIGURE

He won't again, dear person.

NERA

He's gone to sleep upstairs, thank goodness . . . But in the morning when my spine and head ache, he'll cry . . . We'll have to go out to the grape-arbor and have our bread and hot milk, and he'll ask me such impossible questions, like "Where did we all come from?" and "Will we all meet again after this world is gone?" My dear sir, those are the questions I think about all the time also . . . Old age and extreme youth, you see, think the same things, and the trouble is there are no answers to them . . . People who are occupied with the world and making money and shining in their place don't think of them, and often die of a heart attack in their work so that in all their life except when they were children they never so much as thought of the only things we really care about: "Where are we going?" and "Will we live forever?"

FIGURE

But the world is over, dear person, and so our questions too are no longer . . . here.

NERA

Your voice is simply beautiful—pure song . . . Are you a singer? You're young, too, I can see under your heavy clothing you are only a youth.

(*The figure shakes his head.*)

NERA

Youth is so different from childhood or old age . . . What is its characteristic? Yearning? desire? no sense of time? I've forgotten . . . But childhood and old age are so clear to me . . . we ask those haunting questions.

FIGURE
(kneeling before her)
Dear person, the entire world has come to an end, and your questions . . . are no longer necessary . . . If you look up into the firmament, you'll see only one or perhaps two stars, and they're vanishing . . . How you've survived, well, I'm after all, only the . . . *(in a low, low voice)* . . . the *Creator*. Certain things escape one. . . .

NERA
Before you go—I'd like to tell you one thing, except that I feel so . . . so very tired . . . Yet my brain is clear. . . .

FIGURE
I hadn't planned . . . You see, you were spared . . . all unbeknownst even to me.

NERA
Now the question I have in mind seems so absurd when I think twice about it, I don't want to ask it.

FIGURE
(looking around)
There is no light . . . nothing.

NERA
The question I was going to raise is, "Why should we go through the pain of giving birth if it's all going to come to . . . nothing?"

FIGURE
You feel you need an answer?

NERA
I don't think you could answer it in any case. *(hesitant, examining him)* In any real case. *(frightened)* Who are you?

(The figure has stood up and is retreating.)

FIGURE

I must just have a look around before I go. . . .

NERA

Why should you look around? (*indifferent*) Look anywhere you wish, but don't wake the child, and don't say anything to nurse. If she's asleep, good, and if she's loafing at her work, so long as she's quiet, good, also . . . I need some rest, not sleep, rest—rest to all my questions.

FIGURE

Such as *"Why should we go through the pain of giving birth if it's all going to come to . . . nothing?"*

NERA

Did I say that?

FIGURE

Just a moment ago.

NERA

You are still young and have your memory . . . I can recall almost nothing from hour to hour . . . I see the day come, I feel in my bones it is getting later rather than recognize the fact in my mind, and everything is a blur from the present, the immediate past of the day, from the nearer-past, and from the long, long ago. . . .

FIGURE

That's the way it is!

NERA

But the future always seems to end in . . . a blank . . . a question mark. That's what gives one uneasiness . . . You wonder why you've been to all the trouble . . . And yet looking back. . . .

FIGURE

Go on.

NERA

I thought you were going to look around.

FIGURE

I started to, but there was nothing here either, only you. . . .

NERA

My dear . . . Well, if you like to say peculiar things, of course that's your privilege . . . Years ago I would not have liked your way of expressing yourself . . . I would have always admired your voice, because I know you're a singer . . . Perhaps you're in disguise . . . Be that as it may . . . But what was I saying? You see how sad old age is . . . One loses the thread of one's own sentences . . . The day itself merges mindlessly with night . . . But the questions never go away! (*She weeps.*) Why? Why? All the time like a sharp piece of glass in my tired brain . . . They never let up . . . Then I call out to Him who must know all the riddle, and He doesn't say anything . . . I cry all night some times for Him to speak.

FIGURE

"The pain of giving birth—"

NERA

A man like you talking about that . . . with your fine voice . . . When you give birth, you become silent.

FIGURE

I understand.

NERA

Nobody understands but the one who does it . . . You're not a woman.

FIGURE

The whole world has come to an end, and we stand here talking.

NERA

How terrible I will feel in the morning, and nurse or the child will never believe I have sat talking with you all night . . . about nothing. (*She laughs*).

FIGURE

You didn't hear a strange and terrible sound some while ago?

NERA

(*trying to remember*)

Now it is coming back to me . . . yes.

FIGURE

That was it, the end of all.

NERA

(*trying to understand*)

The end of all . . . I see.

FIGURE

But out of it all, you remain . . . You see I had—it was willed—the world would end.

NERA

Oh one of those old, old questions, which, now that old age has come, and I have the child to answer, I think of all the time . . . Insoluble.

FIGURE

When you heard the noise, it was I destroying everything.

NERA

(*looking at him*)

I think you should go away . . . You might frighten the others.

FIGURE

I am going, but I don't know what to do about you . . . Curiously you cannot stay here.

NERA

Your voice was less lovely that time . . . It sounded fatigued . . . A good voice should never allow itself to become tired . . . That was what maternity did to me, among other things, I could no longer sing . . . Yet giving birth was beyond happiness.

FIGURE

That is the way it is!

NERA

Beyond everything.

FIGURE

Yet you voice regret.

NERA

One is always complaining, with eyes shut . . . We destroy our own gifts, one by one . . . Like my children, they left me one by one.

(*As she speaks all her children suddenly appear, a filmy mist over them, near her.*)

NERA

(*moved to ecstasy*)
I say . . . I said . . . (*She is astonished but calm. She stretches out her hand to them.*) Children!

FIGURE

What is it?

NERA

(*As Nera gazes at her children they vanish one by one.*)
It was nothing . . . Memories . . . Lateness of the hour, you see, and when one is old, there are certain little things go wrong with the brain and limb. Yet one is not exactly

mad . . . The body falls to pieces, and the mind, poor
thing, is left without a prop . . . When you said the world
had come to an end, what did you mean a short time ago?

FIGURE
I should not have told you.

NERA
You said the world had come to an end . . . You implied
the child and nurse were not here, if I remember cor-
rectly—or am I dreaming? The nights are so hard on me,
my bones especially seem to revolt against the nights . . .
The body simply falls to pieces, and the mind, poor
thing. . . .

FIGURE
I am only the Creator . . . Beyond that is life, is *is*.

NERA
(*as if quoting*)
"Eternal, renewing itself, coming to itself again and again
long after the pain of giving birth . . ." Are those my
words? "Ending and beginning and continuing and ever-
lasting."

FIGURE
They are life's. . . . (*He starts to go.*)

NERA
Look here, you're leaving, and I have no idea who you
are . . . What if you've escaped from some institution . . .
You're all bundled up in queer clothes too, though it's
summer . . . Come back here or you'll leave me worried
. . . And you've said such odd things, about the world
coming to an end . . . Are you a young man who's escaped
from an institution? Answer me!

FIGURE
(with colorless honesty)
I am the Creator.

NERA
(convinced despite herself)
Forgive me . . . Forgive. . . .

FIGURE
Nothing to forgive, dear person.

NERA
My mind wanders . . . I should have been reverent.

FIGURE
You were . . . you are . . . If it was I who despaired. . . .

NERA
I was the one who despaired . . . I had only questions.

FIGURE
I said the world had come to an end, and I meant it.

NERA
But didn't I say that? I said there would be no more life
when I wasn't here . . . Didn't I say that? After this life,
I said, what of the future? You see I was confused.

FIGURE
No, no, I despaired . . . As the Creator I despaired, but
then I heard something.

NERA
The child?

FIGURE
(shaking his head)
Something in your voice.

NERA
No, no, I have no voice . . . Now you are confusing me,

you see . . . Again, I ask you: Who are you? Oh, I'm afraid, I'm afraid. And you're all bundled up!

FIGURE

The world has commenced again after ending . . . I had ordered it ended, but it was created and therefore was something more than I, even I. It was I and it was more than I.

NERA

Who are you now? You're all bundled up, and you're making fun of me, saying I have a voice . . . It's you who have the voice . . . You're a singer, that's what I said when I first saw you, and it's what I say now . . . You're a beautiful singer, though why you're bundled up—but then you're an opera singer! Of course . . . And you're going!

FIGURE

The Creator is not all, his created go on and they will never stop, they will never, never. . . . (*He goes out.*)

NERA

They will never stop? You did say . . . you were the Creator . . . The Singer . . . Oh when one's old, the body falls apart, the body, the body, and the poor mind. . . .

(*The nurse has awakened and come to the front.*)

NURSE

Now see what you've done . . . You've wakened both me and the child . . . Can't you hear him sqwawking?

NERA

But I've had a visitor!

NURSE

You will sleep in your chair and you have bad dreams . . . Oh you're naughty, naughtier than the child, and I have all the work to do. See my poor hands, they're bleeding from work.

NERA

But you're alive . . . You're alive.

NURSE

You're coming down with some illness, babbling like this.

CHILD

(*rushing in*)
My milk and bread!

NERA

Oh thank God, thank God. (*She embraces the child.*) We'll go right into the grape-arbor and have our hot milk and bread.

NURSE

But the dawn's only just coming. It's still nearly dark and the stars are blinking. You woke us all up too early.

NERA

You heard me, nurse. The child and I will go into the grape-arbor and you will bring our bread and hot milk . . . You see, I dreamed the world and creation had come to an end . . . But just when my despair was at its height. . . .

NURSE

Well, well.

NERA

I can't remember . . . Isn't it awful to be old, the body. . . .

NURSE

Yes, yes, "the body breaks down and then the poor mind."

NERA

The Creator said to me, as I am sitting here, I swear to you—

CHILD

We'll go to the grape-arbor, nice person?

NERA

He said—now I must remember before it's too late, the Creator, that was this young man with the singer's voice covered up with heavy wraps, he said to me, "No matter what the pain of giving birth and the thought that if you would say DON'T BE, DON'T EXIST . . ." Oh my poor mind . . . You see. . . .

NURSE

What are you talking about?

NERA

I must remember what the Creator said . . . You see, it was the answer to all my questions, but I can't remember now . . . You see, as I sat here, he had thought he had destroyed the world, and then, seeing me, hearing me talk, with his own beautiful voice he changed his mind and pronounced the truth.

CHILD

We want our bread and hot milk in the grape-arbor!

NERA

Just a minute now, it's coming . . . I must remember what the Creator said. I will know in a moment and then I'll remember the truth.

NURSE

But you've been dreaming.

NERA

If the body would only let me, but I'm old, old.

CHILD

I want to go to the grape-arbor . . . I must have the milk.

NERA

Now it's coming to me, at last, at last it's coming . . . (*She stands up and looks out over the audience.*)

(*The voice of the figure is heard in the background.*)

FIGURE

"After all the pain of giving birth. . . ."

NERA

That's it, I hear his special voice now.

FIGURE

"After all the pain of creation, the created will continue, after all the pain, after all the pain . . . no matter what we do or say . . . ."

NERA

Creation! That's it. That's the answer to my question . . . Oh don't you hear his voice, my dears . . . The world does not come to an end, no matter how great the pain or the loss . . . You see my question's answered . . . We can go into the grape-arbor now.

CURTAIN